ALL ALONE

"Help!" I finally screamed. My voice echoed against the watching buildings, until it became an echo of an echo, and was lost. I buried my face in my hands, thankful that they at least had not deserted me. Tears filled my eyes, and I cried, but only quietly and to myself because there was no one there to share them with. I was not merely confused. I was lost. Lost in a town I had lived in all my life.

Time did not go by. That would have been a joke. Time had already packed its bags and left town. But something passed and then after a while I became aware that someone was standing above me. I raised my eyes. I had to look into the sun to see him. Just like the first time. Just as I'd looked into the rising sun when I spotted the lone hitchhiker on the empty highway.

"Pepper," I said.

"Where is everybody?" he asked.

Books by Christopher Pike

Christopher Pike

Whisper of Death

AN ARCHWAY PAPERBACK
Published by POCKET BOOKS

New York   London   Toronto   Sydney   Tokyo   Singapore

AN ARCHWAY PAPERBACK *Original*

An Archway Paperback published by
POCKET BOOKS, a division of Simon & Schuster Inc.
1230 Avenue of the Americas, New York, NY 10020

ISBN: 0-671-69058-2

First Archway Paperback printing December 1991

10 9 8 7 6 5 4

AN ARCHWAY PAPERBACK and colophon are registered trademarks of Simon & Schuster Inc.

Cover art by Brian Kotzky

Printed in the U.S.A.

IL 9+

For Carol

Whisper of Death

I SIT ALONE IN A DEAD WORLD. THE WIND BLOWS HOT AND dry, and the dust gathers like particles of memory waiting to be swept away. I pray for forgetfulness, yet my memory remains strong, as does the outstretched arm of the oppressive air. It seems as if the wind has been there since the beginning of the nightmare. Sometimes loud and harsh, a thousand sharp needles scratching at my reddened skin. Sometimes a whisper, a curious sigh in the black of night, of words more frightening than pain. I know now the wind has been speaking to me. Only I couldn't understand because I was too scared. I am scared now as I write these words. Still, there is nothing else to do.

I don't know where to start, but there must be a place. A place of love, of hope. He gave me those things, and others as well. Yes, I will start with him.

His name was Pepper. That wasn't his real name, of course. His parents had christened him Paul Pointzel. He didn't have dark freckles or anything—I don't know where he got his nickname. But he was Pepper when I met him, and that's how I think of him. Pepper and Rox. My name is Roxanne Wells. I'm eighteen, or rather, I was eighteen. At the moment I'm not going to get any older. The second hand on my watch will move forward but won't go anywhere for me. This moment is all there is.

We met in high school. He was a babe. I don't know why he asked me out. I wasn't very nice to him. He was new to the area, but not that new. I'd seen him around town for a year or so before he made a move on me. I'd heard good and bad things about him. One friend said he was just out for sex. Another said he was a romantic at heart. What the hell, I thought. I needed sex and romance in my life. Sometimes I believe I would have taken one without the other. Even before Pepper cornered me I decided that, if given the chance, I would let him get to know me.

It was lunchtime at school, a hot early April afternoon. I was sitting by myself on a rock at the corner of campus staring out at the desert. It was a favorite spot for me to hang out and eat junk food. School was in Salem, Arizona, a town built on sand with a lot of sweat. I had grown up surrounded by an ocean of dust, yet the sight of the desert never tired me. I was always glad the city architects had put Salem High at the edge of town, and not in the center. Downtown Salem was about as exciting as an empty movie theater. Things may have been happening in town, but hardly anyone was there to acknowledge the fact. Even before the transformation, Salem felt barren.

Pepper suddenly appeared, standing above me with his thumbs hooked into the back pockets of his Levi 505s. He was trying to look cool, and not doing a bad job of it. He was too handsome. By that I mean I wasn't given any chance to dislike him. Everything that happened between us had to be. It was inevitable. His hair was brown and messy. He needed a shave. His eyes were as dark as blue prairie grass before a storm. He had a body, every guy does, but his fit him better than most. But I didn't smile at him, not right away. I was cool, too.

"Hey, Roxanne," he said, then paused. "That is your name?"

"It had better be." I had to shield my eyes to look at him. He had the sun behind him, which I think was a strategic move on his part. "What do you want?"

"Got a cigarette?"

"I don't smoke," I said.

"I've seen you smoke."

"When?"

"At the park, at night."

"Those weren't cigarettes," I said.

"To each his own. I'm a beer man myself."

I shrugged, going back to my Honey Bun. "I get loaded once in a blue moon." I took a bite of my bun. "And every Tuesday."

"Mind if I sit down?" he asked, not waiting for my permission to share the rock. At least now I didn't have to blind myself to look at him. "What's so special about Tuesdays?" he asked.

"Tuesday means Monday's over."

He glanced back at campus—the lackadaisical crowd. "You're a senior, aren't you? You'll be out of here pretty soon. What are you going to do after graduation?"

I laughed. "Look at you. We haven't even been

introduced and you want to know what I'm going to do with the rest of my life."

He just stared at me a moment. Then he offered me his hand. "My name's Pepper," he said.

"That's a weird name." I shook his hand. "Is it a nickname?"

"I guess. I hear everyone calls you Rox."

"Only my friends."

"What should I call you?" he asked.

"You don't have to call me anything."

"You're a real sweetheart, you know that?"

I smiled sweetly. "Thank you. Is that a personal observation or is that something else you've heard?"

"Do you want me to leave?"

"Whatever gave you that idea?" I asked.

He stood. "Have a nice lunch, Roxanne."

I quickly put a hand on his knee. "You may call me Rox, Pepper."

He hesitated, then sat back down and stared at the ground. Guys often do that—I don't know why. There's nothing there. "I'm not trying to hit on you or anything," he said.

"What are you trying to do?"

He glanced over. "I was just looking for a cigarette."

"There's a liquor store over on Stills. It sells them. It sells beer as well."

That got him mad. "Do you want me to stay or not?"

I laughed. "I don't know. Now that I know you're not going to hit on me, probably not."

The tension was broken. He laughed, too. "What are you doing next Tuesday?"

Like I said, I was game. "Drinking beer with you. Maybe."

There was no maybe about it. We went out the following Tuesday. It was the only day I didn't have to work, besides Sunday, which was never any good because it came before blue Monday. I was a seamstress in a clothes store. It was boring. I never really got to make dresses, just sewed the seams. It paid zip, like every other teen job in Salem. Pepper had a job, too. I'd seen him at it before we met. He delivered flowers. What a joke. He rode to work on a motorcycle at eighty miles an hour in black leather, then put on a pansy coat and climbed in a van and tooled around Salem making young and old women alike ecstatic. He said the tips weren't bad, and the women were always happy to kiss him.

We went to a movie and I rode on the back of his motorcycle. It was a horror film about the second expedition to Mars called *The Season of Passage*. At the end I wanted to cry because it was so sad, but Pepper was still eating his popcorn. He was stuffing it into his face, and I found it impossible to weep with someone eating beside me.

We went for a malt and fries afterward—a typical date in Salem. The place wasn't option city. We drank a couple of beers on a dark bus stop bench. But then, on the way home, still on the back of his bike, I leaned my head back and gazed at the stars, bright in the clear black sky. I said something to Pepper about wishing we had a flying saucer so we could leave the planet and he instantly made a sharp U turn.

"Where are we going?" I called into the breeze. He drove fast but smooth, with complete control. On our next date, though, I had already decided that we'd go in my car. I liked my hair to look like something naturally attached to my body when I got to where I was going. And I knew there would be a second date. I liked him too much for there not to be.

"To get a telescope," he answered.

"Who has a telescope?"

"Our school."

We ended up breaking into the science lab. It was easy—we just went up a tree and through a window. I had never taken astronomy. I was more the basic education kind of girl. Give me my diploma and I'd be gone. The telescope sat on a collapsible tripod. Pepper hoisted it onto his shoulder and walked toward the door. He assured me we'd bring it back when we were done with it and nobody would even know it had been on a vacation.

"Where are we going with it?" I asked. I didn't mind a little adventure.

"To the reservoir."

That sounded fine to me except for the obvious. "But we're on a motorcycle," I said.

"It's not that big a telescope, Rox."

"What else are we going to do at the reservoir?" I asked, suspicious.

He cocked an eyebrow. "Nothing you won't enjoy."

"I'm not that kind of girl."

"They all say that."

I socked him. "Some of us mean it."

But I don't know if I was one of them. We didn't have sex the first night anyway. We had a hard enough time getting the telescope out to the reservoir. Pepper complicated matters by roaring through the center of town so that everyone could see what we were doing. I almost dropped the damn thing a half dozen times.

The reservoir was cool, especially at night, when the water was like glass and the air was filled with space. You could stand out there alone at night, with the Milky Way streaming over head, and imagine you were standing on a moon circling Saturn. Pepper had never taken astronomy either, so we had a hard time finding anything specific. Yet, to me, everywhere we looked there was something. Stars, thousands of stars. It made me wish I was an astronaut, a Goddess, anything but a poor girl in a poor town with no future. I sighed as I removed my eye from the telescope eyepiece.

"Do you think there's anyone out there?" I asked Pepper, my eyes staring straight up.

"No one human." He came up behind me and put his hands on my shoulders. I leaned back and rested my head in the hollow of his shoulder. The night was magic, the silence perfect. I was happy right then, really happy, but sad, too, because I knew the happiness wouldn't last. It never does.

"Would that be so bad?" I asked, my gaze millions of light-years away, his breath warm and close on my cheek.

"What do you mean?" he asked.

"Would it be so bad if they weren't human—as long as they were kind?"

He pulled me around gently until I was facing him. "You're beautiful, Rox. You deserve a sky full of kind stars."

I laughed lightly. "Don't talk. You sound stupid when you do."

"What should I do then?"

"Kiss me."

He kissed me. I made him do it. It was good, too good.

He took me back to the reservoir that Friday night after work. We didn't bring the telescope, but we had the place to ourselves again. We skinny-dipped in the cool water. We kissed some more, and I let him touch my breasts, but we didn't make love. Or maybe we did make love because I was already in love with him. I don't know why. The best love never has a reason. I just had to look at him and there was no reason to look anywhere else.

Pepper lived with his aunt and uncle. I lived with my dad. Dad was never at home. He was a long-distance truck driver. He drove from New York to L.A., and back again, every week. We had a peculiar relationship. I was more his pal than his daughter. When he was home I cleaned his clothes and fed him, but the way we talked to each other would have made a child psychologist cringe. We argued, we swore at each other, and in the end he usually agreed with me. But we loved each other, too. His name was Sam.

I never knew my mother. From the things Sam had

to say, it didn't sound like he knew her very well, either. She left on a westbound Greyhound bus when I was forty-eight hours old. Seemed she wanted to be an actress in Hollywood, or something.

Pepper's aunt and uncle lived on the other edge of town from the school, on a miserable farm better known for its horses than its produce. But like any farm, good or bad, it had a barn. And it was in that barn that I lost my virginity after a thorough examination by Dr. Pepper.

I don't really remember how the date started. We ate, I know that, but I can't remember where. Then we went for a long walk, and in Salem, it's not possible to walk too far without coming back home. We ended up at Pepper's place. His aunt and uncle were asleep. Pepper wanted to show me his horse, Shadowfax, named after Gandalf the wizard's horse in *The Lord of the Rings*. It was a nice horse. It was a nice barn, full of nice, soft hay.

But there was something wicked inside that hay that almost got me killed. When we began to kiss, Pepper suddenly tickled me, and I fell back and landed on the hay. I missed impaling myself on a pitchfork by inches. Pepper was white when I pulled it out of the straw beside me.

"Did you set this up?" I asked, the pitchfork in my hand, pointed at him. "I can see the headlines now. Poor innocent coed pierced on the eve of greatness."

Pepper grabbed the pitchfork from my hand and tossed it aside. He wiped the sweat off his forehead. I could tell he was shaken. He came and knelt beside me and spoke seriously.

"You are great," he said.

I grinned. Those three little words meant more to me than those other famous three little words—I think. He had yet to say those words, and I was determined not to say them until he said them to me.

"Why?" I asked. "I'm not pretty. I'm not smart. I'm nothing."

Yet I knew I wasn't ugly or stupid. My hair was long and red, my eyes green and bright—a nice combination. I was too thin—I had no tits—but even girlfriends complimented me on my legs. Those same girls, however, said I didn't smile enough. Melancholy Rox. I didn't like to smile because of my teeth. They were crooked, and didn't shine like those of the actresses on TV.

I also seldom smiled because I felt haunted and cursed.

Like it was only a matter of time.

But for what I didn't know.

But in the barn, with my Pepper sitting beside me, the curse seemed oh so far away—when actually it had never been closer. Maybe I was stupid.

"You're something," Pepper said, taking my hand.

"What?" I asked.

He moved closer. "What do you want to be?"

"Happy."

He snorted, and scanned the hay, perhaps to determine how flammable it was. "Do you have a cigarette?" he asked.

"That's what you said when we met. You're not supposed to say that right now."

"No?"

"A cigarette's supposed to be for after."

He moved close, close enough to kiss. "After what, Rox?"

I was looking at the stars in his eyes, the ones I had put there. And I was looking far away. Like I said, he was too cute. My determination wavered. I had no choice but to say what I did.

"I love you," I whispered.

The words seemed to worry him, like when I had missed the pitchfork, which had only made me smile. I wished so much that he would smile right then.

"Why?" he asked.

"Because it makes me happy." I hesitated. "Do you love me?"

Now I had put him on the spot. He was really missing his cigarette. But he didn't look away. He kissed me instead, lightly, and then sneezed in his lap. I had to laugh.

"Never mind," I said.

He shook his head. "It's not you. It's the hay."

I lifted my knee and poked him with my foot. "I like this hay. It's like one giant bed."

That was a hint he understood. The way he looked at me changed. It wasn't a lustful look. It was more like his worry deepened and transformed inside him, becoming something closer to fear. But being scared can be fun, and he looked interested, too. He took me in his arms.

"What do you want to do?" he asked.

I brushed his hair back. "What comes easiest."

"Rox . . ." he began. I closed his lips with my finger. "Shh. You don't have to say it."

11

"I love you, too."

"I told you," I began. He closed off my lips, with his finger.

"I will love you," he corrected himself. "Is that good enough?"

I nodded, feeling the hay at the back of my neck, sliding down my shirt. "Yeah. Just don't wait too long."

"I won't," he promised.

And then, just before it all began, and the train raced down the hill to the bottom, I asked him one question. I didn't want to. His answer stood a fifty percent chance of ruining everything. But I had to ask it. I stared at the pitchfork as I spoke, lying so innocently beside us.

"Is this your first time?" I asked.

"Is it yours?"

"Yes."

He kissed the side of my face. "It's my first time, too, Rox."

I cannot talk too much about the sex. It was better than ice cream. It was like a summer night before summer really began, before school let out. For me anticipation has always been stronger than the reality, and this was such rich anticipation, so constant, that it couldn't help but be fulfilled. What I mean is, I was happy in his arms, like I was that night we were together in the arms of the stars. I felt so much a part of him I honestly believed, for a long time afterward, that I could be a part of everything.

Did I think of protection against pregnancy? We only made love that one time. I hardly had a chance to think anything. I suppose the thought of contraceptives crossed my mind after we were done. But that's the same as thinking about your parachute after you've jumped. You can think all you want—the ground doesn't give a damn.

I suspected I was pregnant two weeks later. I wasn't late on my period, not yet, but something inside me had changed. A doctor would have said it was hormonal. Maybe, but it was more than that. *I* had changed, not just my body. But it wasn't like something had been added inside, the way new mothers usually talk. It was more like a part of me had died.

Then another two weeks went by, and my period never came. I didn't tell Pepper. I didn't want to worry him. I went to the drugstore in Lendel—a nearby town—and bought an early pregnancy test. Those suckers cost more than I thought—a big fifteen bucks. I read the instructions carefully. The bottom line was that if it tested negative, then you could still be pregnant. They weren't making any guarantees. But if it tested positive, then you were definitely looking at a major change in lifestyle. I took the test.

I failed it. I mean, I passed it.

I held that pink-colored test tube in my hand and started shaking. But no matter how hard I shook, the test tube didn't turn blue or green.

I was pregnant. God.

I didn't cry. How could I? It was a miracle. It was a gift from God. I threw up instead. Then I got out the Yellow Pages and called a doctor in Lendel. That's what the instructions inside the test box had said to do. Just in case your doctor had a different colored test tube, I guess. I didn't have my own physician. I seldom got sick, and when I did I just waited it out. I called Dr. Adams. He was the first one listed. I spoke to his nurse. She wanted me to have a blood test and a urine test, even before I saw the doctor. I asked how much. Seventy bucks, she replied. My baby was already getting expensive, I thought. I said all right.

I passed these tests. I mean, I *passed* them.

The doctor was finally willing to see me about a week after I called. He was younger than I thought he'd be, and better looking, which made me even more nervous. He didn't make me take off my clothes and examine me. We just sat down in his office. He started off by asking how I felt.

"I'm all right," I said.

"I didn't mean physically. Are you upset? Are you happy?"

"The first choice," I said.

"Do you have a boyfriend?"

"I think so."

"Does he know?"

"No."

"Are you going to tell him?"

"Yes."

"Do you want to keep the baby?" he asked.

It was such a normal question for a doctor to ask, and I know it sounds impossible, but I had never asked myself that question. "I don't know," I said, gesturing helplessly. "I've never been pregnant before."

He was sympathetic. "How old are you, Roxanne?"

"Eighteen."

"You're legal."

"What do you mean?"

"You can make your own choice." He paused. "Have you told your parents?"

"I only have a father. I haven't told him."

He studied me. His brown eyes were kind. "You look like a girl with a head on her shoulders. You know the choices you have?"

I nodded. "There aren't that many of them."

"There's a family planning clinic in Foster. It's a two-hour drive. If you want to go there, you just have to give me a call and I'll set up an appointment for you."

"I don't want to go there," I said so sharply I startled us both. He didn't want to say the word, and I didn't want to hear it, but we were both talking about *abortion*. Just the sound of it in my head made me feel sick. I wished they had given the procedure initials instead of a name. Like, oh, just going to have a ABT. Be back before lunch. Then I could pretend it wasn't much different from ordering a bacon, lettuce, and tomato sandwich.

Dr. Adams stood and squeezed my shoulder. "You think about what you want to do. Talk to your father and your boyfriend if you wish. But don't let anyone make the decision for you. OK?"

"OK. Thank you, doctor."

I paid the nurse at the front and drove home. My car was overheating—I had to stop twice and cool the radiator down with water. It was four in the afternoon on a blue Monday. I knew Pepper was at work, driving around town with his bright floral arrangements. There was no reason I couldn't wait until he was off to tell him the news. After all, I had already waited so long. But I needed a friend. I didn't really have anyone except Pepper. My best friend, Susan Duggin, had moved to Florida the previous year. I realized right then how superficial the rest of my friendships were. My boyfriend was the only one I could imagine myself talking to about my problem.

I caught him as he was loading the last of his deliveries in the van. It was funny—I had never seen him so happy to see me. He gave me a big hug and a kiss, and plucked a rose from an arrangement and fixed it in my hair. All that before I could say a word.

But then I didn't have to say much. He was staring at my face now. If he saw half of what I felt he must have been in shock. I felt sorry for him right then. Heck, I felt sorry for me. We had our whole lives in front of us. The last few days he had been talking about driving to L.A. We'd get a place in Venice by the beach, he said, and walk by the water every evening. I just smiled. It sounded so wonderful. But he didn't even know if he loved me.

"What is it, Rox?" he asked.

"I have some good news and I have some bad news. What do you want to hear first?"

He hesitated. "The good news."

"It's yours."

"What's mine?"

"The bad news."

"What?"

"The baby."

16

He sagged a little. "What are you talking about?" he asked.

"I'm pregnant." I hastily added, "I'm sorry."

He tried to swallow. It stuck somewhere in his throat. Then he just stood there, looking at a distant spot located off to the left side of my eyes. I had never seen anyone's tan fade so fast.

"Are you sure?" he asked softly, finally.

"I just came from the doctor's." I buried my face in his chest, hugging him tightly. I fought the tears back, and it was probably the only fight I had won all day. Only a few weeks had passed since I had mouthed off to him at school. How everything had changed. Falling in love had humbled me to the point of being pathetic. "Do you hate me?" I asked meekly.

He put his arms weakly around me. "No, of course not. Why would I hate you?"

"Because I screwed up."

"No, Rox." He pulled me gently off him, and looked at my face. "You didn't do anything wrong. We'll get through this together, all right?"

"All right." I took out my handkerchief and blew my nose. "What are we going to call her?"

He chuckled—it sounded forced. "How do you know it's a *her?*"

"I just know," I said. And I did. That should have told me that something weird was in the air. "How about if we call her Pebbles? After the baby girl on the Flintstones? Pebbles and Rox."

Pepper wasn't smiling. "Are you serious?"

"We can call her anything you want."

"That's not what I mean, Rox," he said slowly.

My voice faltered. "You don't want to keep the baby?" I asked.

"Do you?"

"I'd like to."

"Why?"

The question hit me like a slap. It took me a moment to find my tongue. "Because it would be our baby."

He had to think about that a bit, and the passing seconds were hard on me. It was an absurd place to be having such a discussion—the dirty back lot of a florist's. I reached up and touched the flower Pepper had placed in my hair, but I was clumsy and it fell to the ground. I knelt to pick it up. Pepper stopped me.

"It's no good," he said.

I was on edge. "What's no good?"

He gestured. "The flower. Leave it. I'll get you another one." But he didn't reach back into the van. I had given him too much to think about, and he couldn't worry about me right then. He continued to stare off into the distance. I had to break the silence.

"It's not like it's fatal," I joked.

"Do you really want to keep the baby?"

I paused. "I thought you just asked me that."

"Rox."

"Do *you* want to keep it? If you don't, just tell me."

"I don't," he said.

I couldn't believe he'd said that. Oh, I knew, of course, he might want me to have an abortion. But for him not to consider having the child made me sad. He didn't even want to sleep on it. But I was no better. I was the child's mother, and all I cared about was

18

remaining his girlfriend. I would throw away the price of love to be in love. My response just came out of my mouth. It was fate that spoke.

"All right," I said.

He held me again. He acted all concerned, but there was something fake about it and we both knew it. "I'll help you in any way I can," he said. "I'll go with you. I'll pay for it."

Then suddenly I was far away. More words came out of my mouth, but I know I did not speak these ones. There was no love in them. There was nothing of what I really felt for Pepper in them. Yet I said them anyway. Because they were supposed to be true.

"I'll get rid of it," I said. "Life will go on."

But it was all a lie.

CHAPTER II

THERE IS MUCH DEBATE IN THIS COUNTRY OVER ABORTION. I have always found it puzzling. There are the right-to-lifers who say that abortion is the equivalent of murder. Then there are those who say a woman's right of free choice must be preserved. What has always struck me as odd is that each side is convinced that only it is right, and the other is wrong.

I feel they are both wrong. No one should take away another person's right to choose. And no one should kill an unborn infant. Of course I could just as easily say both sides are right, but I won't. It's a paradox that can't be resolved. I think it is better to admit that than pretend there is a resolution.

But most people want to believe what they are doing is right. I guess I have always been unique in that respect. I knew smoking dope was a lousy thing to do, but I did it anyway. I knew I should study more, but I couldn't be bothered. I goofed off and got loaded because I wanted to, and that was reason enough. Yet it wasn't as if I had no conscience. These things only hurt me, and I was willing to do them because I could take the hurt. I almost preferred it. Now, though, I had a baby in me. The baby could hurt me. It could drive my boyfriend away. It could make me work and slave for the next eighteen years. I could hurt it. I could kill it. But Dr. Adams assured me it would be a painless death. Without consciousness, there could be no agony, and the doctor said that an immature fetus had zero awareness. I believed him.

Dr. Adams made the appointment for me at the family planning clinic on Saturday in Foster. Because he had already completed all the necessary tests it was not required that I come in beforehand. All I had to do was show up for the procedure. The time was set for five-thirty in the morning. Apparently the surgeons liked to get rid of nasty business early so they could spend the rest of the day saving lives. The cost for the abortion would be four hundred and sixty-two dollars. The clinic wanted to be paid up front. Pepper insisted on covering it all, but I said, no, we'd split it. I only had three hundred dollars in the bank to begin with. Condoms would have been cheaper. A heart transplant would have been easier. All my talk was just talk. As we drove to Foster the night before, Friday, I felt I was driving to my death.

We decided to get a motel in Foster and sleep, but we ended up talking till it was time to go to the clinic. My dad was out of town, and Pepper's aunt and uncle thought he was camping with a friend. The clinic was located in a small professional office building. It was still dark as we parked my car and walked inside. A plump middle-aged woman looked up from behind a gray metal desk. She may have been a nurse; she was all in white. A mole the size of a quarter, complete with fine brown hairs, occupied the left side of her generous chin. There were no other women present.

"Are you Roxanne?" the woman asked.

"Yes. Are we early?" The place was plainly furnished and smelled of alcohol.

"A few minutes." The woman was all business. She reached for a handful of forms. "Fill these out, please. Will you be paying with cash or check?"

"I'll just put it on my expense account," I said.

"Pardon?" the woman said. She had heard me, but didn't like my sense of humor.

"Cash," Pepper said sourly, reaching for his wallet. I knew neither of us had imagined we'd be spending our hard-earned money this way.

I filled out the forms. I had the wild thought in the middle of them that one day I would run for president, and that the forms would be dug up by my opponent, and used to smear my good name. So I changed a few things about myself, including the spelling of my last name, and where I lived, and so on. I mean, it wasn't as if I wanted to receive the clinic's monthly newsletter.

Pepper sat silently beside me as I wrote. If it had been him who was filling out the forms, then I would have probably helped him. He did worse in school than I did. Our child probably would have been retarded, I consoled myself as I finished the papers and gave them back to the mean woman. I was talking to myself a mile a minute, the whole rationalizing trip, but I spoke like someone was listening to me. The baby, of course—I imagined she could hear my mental dialogue. And although she remained silent throughout, I had a sense of how she felt, and the feeling was not pleasant.

A man suddenly appeared in the doorway. He was dressed in a sterile green gown, serious and intimidating. He was over six and a half feet tall, and seated as I was, his covered head looked like something in orbit. He glanced briefly at me before his eyes moved to the woman behind the desk.

"I'm ready for our first patient, Carol," he said.

Then he closed the door, and was gone. The woman lumbered up from behind her desk. "Come this way," she said.

I stood, Pepper with me. We hugged each other briefly. "It'll all be over before you know it," he said.

"I know." I pressed my mouth to his ear, whispering, "Love you."

"Rox—" he began.

"Best we hurry," the woman interrupted.

I let go of Pepper. "Goodbye," I said.

"I'll be right here when you come out," he promised.

We entered a different door from the one the doctor had disappeared behind. The smell of alcohol thickened. The clinic was small. A few steps and we were in the operating room. The woman handed me a green gown and told me to undress completely and lie on the table with my feet up in the stirrups. I could not believe this was happening. The woman left the room and I began to unbutton my blouse. What a way to begin a relationship, I thought.

I was lying on the table with my legs crossed when the doctor entered the room a few minutes later. I wanted to tell him that the table was making my bare butt cold. I also wanted to tell him that I was basically a good person who had made a mistake and that I didn't mean anybody any harm, particularly to the many tiny babies of the world. But I didn't say anything. He gently took hold of my feet and placed them in the stirrups.

"I'm going to give you a series of shots, Roxanne," he said. "It will numb the area."

"Will they hurt?" I asked.

"Yes. But only for a moment."

"I like an honest doctor."

He reached for a packet on a nearby shelf and opened it. There was a long needle inside and a small bottle of clear liquid next to it. He stabbed the needle into the top of the bottle and slowly filled the syringe, holding it up to the light. It looked like Excalibur, I thought, and he was going to stick it into me.

"Jesus," I whispered.

"Don't be afraid," he said.

I chuckled. "It was more fun getting into this predicament than it is getting out of it."

He smiled at my comment, but only for a moment. He wasn't a bad man, but I was just another girl in trouble to him. He probably saw hundreds a year, if not thousands. This was business to him, not a matter of life or death. It was only then I wondered if an abortion could be dangerous. I remembered one of the forms I signed had said something about not holding the clinic responsible in the event I croaked.

He gave me the shots. They hurt like hell. My eyes were wet when he finished. Then he started an I.V. into my wrist and patted my arm and told me he would be back in fifteen minutes. I could hear a girl in the adjacent room undressing. It did not make me feel any less lonely.

The gown was drafty and the doctor had left the door open. I tried to pass the time by singing softly. People told me I had an incredible voice, but I didn't believe them. I always just sounded like myself. I quickly had to give up on the ploy. No one had written a getting-ready-for-my-abortion song.

Time crept by. Deep inside I felt things going numb. The doctor finally returned and poked at me with glove-covered fingers. I told him I couldn't feel a thing and this made him happy. He was ready to begin the procedure. He picked up a long sharp silver instrument that glinted in the harsh overhead light. I closed my eyes.

He poked me again and then suddenly muttered something under his breath and left the room in a hurry. I kept my eyes closed. My guts felt strange, as if they were made of liquid, and were flowing around inside me. My thoughts began to float inside my head, too, like colored pictures projected on puffy white clouds caught in a gentle updraft. I thought mainly of Salem, where I had grown up, and how bright the stars had been the night Pepper had first kissed me.

But the thought of Betty Sue McCormick also flashed inside, her face spread across my imaginary black sky. It was odd that Betty Sue should come to mind. I had hardly known her. Hers was a sad tale. She had doused herself with gasoline in an abandoned gas station at the edge of town, and then she dropped a flaming match at her feet. The whole place had gone up, and there hadn't been much left of Betty Sue to bury. No one knew why she had done it.

Just the thought of Betty Sue, though, and how she had thrown away her life, got me thinking about my baby, and what I was doing to it. My inner resolve to go ahead with the abortion suddenly turned over sharply inside me. Why was I doing this? Had I really asked myself that question? If I had, I had forgotten the answer to it. Yeah, sure, Pepper wanted me to get rid of the kid, and I was worried about losing Pepper. But if he was going to leave me now for this reason, he would leave me later for another. I had nothing to lose, I thought, by keeping what was ours.

I wanted to stop the procedure. I wanted to go home.

"Doctor?" I called, opening my eyes. "Are you there?"

No answer. I pulled my right leg out of the stirrup, then my left. I could sense that I was still numb inside, but believed I could walk. I didn't think I'd changed my mind too late. The doctor had only worked on me a few minutes before leaving. I could see no blood, and suddenly my sensation of dizziness vanished. I felt good, better in fact than I had since I found out I was pregnant. I swung my legs over the side of the table and stood up.

I called out to the doctor and nurse again. Still no answer. The green gown was bugging me, so I pulled it off and quickly slipped back into my clothes. Then I stepped into the hallway.

A dizzy sensation overtook me with a bang.

As I looked down the hall, opposite the direction from which I had entered the operating room, the walls suddenly elongated, stretching the hall into what could have been a pathway into infinity. At the very end of the hall was blackness. Nothingness. I shot out my right arm and caught the edge of the door frame with my hand. I passed the back of my hand over my eyes and steadied myself. My vision cleared. The length of the hallway shrunk to normal size. I turned and walked toward the reception area.

Pepper jumped up as I came out. He had been reading a *People* magazine. The woman at the desk must have been in the back. We were alone.

"Are you done already?" he asked.

"Yes."

"You weren't in there long."

"I'm a quick fix." I opened the door to the outside. Faint blue light shone in the east. "Let's get out of here."

Pepper hurried after me. "Are you sure you're all right?"

"I'm perfect," I said stepping outside into the cool morning air. "Give me the keys. I want to drive."

"Rox, you can't. You just had an operation."

I paused on the opposite side of the car from him. "I didn't do it."

"You didn't have the abortion?" he asked, shocked.

"No. And I don't want to argue about it."

"Rox?"

I put up my hand. "I just want to go home, OK? Give me the keys."

He tossed me the keys, reluctantly. We climbed in the car and drove away. I half expected the ugly fat nurse to come bursting out of the clinic shouting for us to stop. But we left in silence.

And the silence followed us.

"I think we should talk about this," Pepper said softly, five minutes later when we were on the out-skirts of Foster. The town was twice the size of Salem, but that wasn't saying it was big. Soon we would be in the desert.

"I've decided to have the baby," I said calmly. "We can talk all you want. I think you're right—we should talk. But I'm not going to change my mind. If that's not all right with you, I understand. You won't have to be responsible for raising our daughter. If you don't pay child support, I won't take any kind of legal action against you. You'll be free to live your life exactly as you want."

He stared at me for a while before responding. I couldn't see his expression—I could only glimpse him out of the corner of my eye. I had my eyes on the road. We seemed to be the only ones leaving Foster that morning.

"How do you know it's a girl?" he asked again.

I chuckled. "I'm not sure—I just know."

"Nothing I say will make any difference?"

"Nope."

He sighed, settling himself in the seat as if he were about to take a nap. "Then I won't say anything, except that I'll see you through this."

I glanced over at him. "That makes a difference," I said.

Pepper nodded, and then fell asleep. Men, boys—they could sleep through the end of the world. Of course we had been up the entire night before. I never knew Pepper snored. I thought it was cute.

When the sun came up an hour later, Pepper was still asleep. The sun peeked over the horizon directly in front of me and burned bright into my brain. It was at that exact moment that I saw a hitchhiker at the side of the road about half a mile in front of us. It looked like a girl, but I couldn't have sworn to it. It might have been a guy with long, red hair, brighter than mine. The person had on a long dark cape, but framed against the light of the sun, she was little more than a silhouette with flaming hair. I debated whether I'd pick her up. I usually did pick people up.

I assumed the person was hitchhiking. But as I raised my hand to shield my eyes from the glare, she disappeared. There was a cluster of cactuses just off the road. I assumed she had seen us coming and ducked behind them. I wasn't going to worry about it. I had enough on my mind. I drove by the spot she had been standing without slowing one bit.

An hour later, about five miles outside of Salem, I

came to a familiar gas station. I glanced down at my gauge. I was on my last half gallon. I decided to stop and fill up. Pulling into the station beside the pump, I reached over and shook Pepper gently. He hadn't stirred once since we'd left Foster.

"Hey, sleepyhead," I said. "We're almost home."

He opened his eyes and yawned. "What time is it?"

"Almost eight. We need gas. Do you have any money?"

He closed his eyes again. "The clinic has all my money."

I got out. "Thanks."

"Just stating the facts, miss."

Like I said, I knew the station. It was always open. You could pump your gas before paying. I dug a mangled five-dollar bill out of my blue jeans. I wouldn't be filling up, after all. Pepper was snoring again before I got my four point three gallons in the tank. I walked up to the window to pay. A faint breeze played with my hair. The sky was as blue as summer. I knew it was going to be a cooker of a day.

There was no one at the window, although it was open.

"Hello? Anyone home?"

No answer. The garage doors were pulled down, but the cash register was lying open. That was odd, I thought. Even if the guy on duty had had to go to the bathroom, he would have closed the cash register. Immediately I thought the place was being held up. The help was in the back with a bullet in the brain and the villain was this very moment returning for the cash. I backed away from the window three steps, then whirled around and ran for the car.

"Pepper," I said quietly. "Wake up. We have to get out of here."

He didn't open his eyes or sit up. "The car runs just as well with me asleep as it does with me awake."

I opened the car door. "I think this place is being held up."

He bolted upright and glanced at the window. "Why?"

"I called and no one answered. The cash register's lying open."

"The guy could be in the bathroom."

I climbed in the car. "I don't think so. I have a bad feeling about this. I want to get out of here." I put the key in the ignition. Pepper put a hand on my arm.

"Wait a sec," he said. "If the place is being held up we should help."

"We can't help. Only people with loaded guns can help in situations like this. Let's go!"

"No," Pepper said. "That wouldn't be cool."

"I don't want to be cool. I want to be alive. Let go of my arm!"

He opened his door. "You stay here. I'll be back in a moment. If you hear gunshots, drive off."

I grabbed his arm. "Oh, sure. Oh, great. What a classic macho attitude. You are coming with me. My daughter is not going to grow up without a father."

"It could be a boy, for Christsakes." He shook loose. "Do as I say—and don't worry."

"I won't worry," I said sarcastically, sitting back.

"I'll take these few moments to enjoy a peaceful meditation." He closed the door in my face. I pounded the dashboard. "Dammit!"

I watched as he walked casually up to the window. One thing about Pepper—he was no coward. He peered in the window, listened for a second, and then walked around the side of the building to a door and disappeared inside. Why did I go to an abortion clinic and pay them four hundred bucks? I just had to sit through a holdup and I'd abort. I clasped my hand over my abdomen and waited. I didn't start the car. If someone shot Pepper, I thought, they could shoot me as well.

He was back a minute later. I was so relieved I almost started crying. "There's no one here," he said.

"Are you sure?"

"Positive. There's no one in the back, the bathrooms, anywhere."

"Why would they just go off and leave the money lying around like that?"

Pepper was puzzled. "I don't know "

I handed him my five-dollar bill. "Well, stick this in their cash register and let's get out of here."

Pepper stuffed the money in his jeans pocket and climbed inside. "Gimme a break," he said.

"That's stealing."

"Yeah, well, turn me in when we get to town."

"You're mad at me," I said.

"I'm not mad at you."

"Then why don't you talk to me?" I asked.

"Because you told me talking to you would be a

waste of time. Then I went to sleep, and I don't talk in my sleep."

"You snore, though."

"I don't snore," he said.

"Yeah, you do. I don't mind. I know it's beyond your control."

"Thank you, Rox. Now can we get out of here. This place is giving me the creeps."

I paused. "Why did you say that?"

"Rox."

"No." I glanced at the deserted window again. "There *is* something creepy about this place. Can you feel it?"

"It's just because it's deserted, that's all."

"But why is it deserted?"

"I told you, I don't know why. Please, let's go home."

I started the car reluctantly. "OK."

We drove into Salem. There was no one out. It was no big deal. It was still early. But it was odd. We went to Pepper's house. He climbed out of the car without giving me a goodbye kiss.

"What are your plans today?" I asked him.

"I want to sleep some more."

"And after that? Do you want to get together? I have the whole day free." I'd made sure I had the day off so I could recover from my operation. I was recovering all right. In nine months I would be fully healed.

"Sure," he said without enthusiasm. He turned away.

"Pepper?"

He stopped with his back to me. "I told you, I understand."

"I'm sorry."

He sighed and glanced over his shoulder. "I hope we're not both sorry."

"Yeah," I agreed.

I drove home. On the way I noticed again how quiet the town was. There should have been someone on the road. I couldn't even hear a bird singing. Yeah, I noticed the silence, but it didn't make me wonder. I was more amazed at how wide awake I felt. It was a while since I'd slept.

I parked in the driveway and went inside. Like I said, my dad was out of town. Yet the moment I stepped through the door I was struck by how empty the house felt—as if no one had ever lived there.

"Dad?" I called. Of course no one answered. I think I just wanted to hear the sound of my voice. My jitters from the deserted gas station were still with me. I went into the kitchen and put on a pot of coffee. I drank a dozen cups a day. I would have to learn to cut down. The caffeine wouldn't be good for the baby.

While waiting for the coffee, I flipped on the radio. I had just bought it the previous month. It was a Sony, and had twin cassette players and excellent reception.

Only static came out of the speakers.

I leaned over and checked the dial. It was tuned to my favorite station—98.7 "Rock You Until You Go to Heaven." Crazy Harry should have been greasing up the airwaves by now, I thought. I fiddled with the dial. The static continued. I switched to another station. More fuzz.

"Damn," I muttered. "He told me it was the better model."

I turned off the radio. My coffee was ready. I take it black, with both sugar and Sweet 'N' Low. I mixed myself a powerful hit and sat in my dad's favorite chair in the living room, sipping and thinking. Our house would be nothing to film a movie inside. We had only two box bedrooms and one bathroom that would probably be reincarnated as an outhouse. Still, it was cozy enough. My dad painted in oils in his spare time, when his back wasn't killing him from all his driving. He favored mountain scenes copied from National Geographic photographs. His works covered the walls around me.

But the silence, the emptiness—it seemed to seep into me from the floor. I couldn't explain it. I set my coffee down and walked over and turned on the TV.

Static. Fuzz.

"Like the radio," I whispered.

I flipped through the channels. Nothing.

"Oh, no," I said.

Suddenly I was afraid. Afraid of nothing, that most awful of fears. Especially when nothing is all there is.

I strode over to the window and looked out. I watched for five minutes and not a single car drove by. My fear deepened as the silence around me seemed to expand. The only sound was the faint rustling of the wind on the walls of the house, the desert sand scratching at the paint, like long nails craving an invitation inside.

I sat back in my dad's favorite chair and picked up the phone. The dial tone was reassuring. I dialed

Pepper's number. It rang and rang. I called a friend at school, Sandy Hankins. There was no answer. I called the local supermarket. It was open twenty-four hours a day. Nobody home. I called my best friend, Susan Duggin, in Florida. I got her parents' answering machine. I put down the phone and thought of the deserted gas station. Even before we got into town . . .

"Where is everybody?" I asked out loud.

No one answered me. I almost screamed right then. I would have but the silence wouldn't allow it. The silence was too strong. I got up and ran out of the house.

The block was deserted. I went to my neighbors— the Hollens. They had two hyperactive kids and a dog that barked at its own barking. I banged on the door.

"Hello! Is anyone there? Please answer if you're there. It's an emergency."

I was talking to a door. I ran to my neighbors on the other side—the Blaines. No kids or animals but two loud people who got up early and let the rest of the world know it. I called to them, too, and injured their front door with my fists, but they were definitely not home.

It seemed no one was.

What did I do next? I began to move toward the center of town—six blocks away. I stopped at other houses, even peeked my head in a couple, but I quit doing it very soon. There was no one around. The sight of a corpse would have been welcome to me right then. A skeleton, sitting at a kitchen table with a fresh cup of steaming coffee. Sure, let me meet him, I'm desperate. Anything, even a goldfish. But I was alone.

I stumbled into the town square and collapsed on the lawn beside the statue of David Fitzpatrick—the town's founding father. He was covered with bird lime, as usual, but there were no birds. They must have all flown away, into a sky above mine.

"Help!" I finally screamed. My voice echoed against the watching buildings, until it became an echo of an echo, and was lost. I buried my face in my hands, thankful that they at least had not deserted me. Tears filled my eyes, and I cried, but only quietly and to myself because there was no one there to share them with. I was not merely confused. I was lost. Lost in a town I had lived in all my life.

Time did not go by. That would have been a joke. Time had already packed its bags and left town. But something passed, and then after a while I became aware that someone was standing above me. I raised my eyes. I had to look into the sun to see him. Just like the first time. Just as I'd looked into the rising sun when I spotted the lone hitchhiker on the empty highway.

"Pepper," I said.

"Where is everybody?" he asked.

CHAPTER III

PEPPER TOLD ME HIS STORY. HIS AUNT AND UNCLE HAD BEEN out when he'd gone into the house. The fact hadn't disturbed him greatly, but when he had lain down to sleep, the creepy feeling he'd felt at the gas station wouldn't go away. He got up and called me, but I must have already been out and pounding on the neighbors' doors. He called a few friends, but no one was home. He didn't turn on the radio or TV, but started walking toward the center of town as I had done, calling out for anyone to answer. Finally, of course, he found me.

We sat on a bench in the center of the town square as we caught up on each other's stories. To say there was a feeling of unreality to our situation would have been like saying the sun was hot. We sat on a bench in the shade, but we were perspiring. Both our shirts were stained with cold sweat.

"Why would everyone leave?" I asked.

Pepper grimaced and sat quietly thinking. "The only thing I can figure is there must have been some kind of evacuation. Maybe there was a toxic spill in the area. The National Guard could have been brought in last night. They might have cleared every-one out."

"If that was the case they'd have put up road-blocks."

He nodded. "I know. But it's the only explanation that makes any kind of sense. There were people here at nine last night when we left. Now they're gone. There must be a reason. There must be something bad here. I think we better get the hell out of here."

"But I told you how I called Susan in Florida. Even she wasn't home. It's like everybody's disappeared."

"Are you saying the whole world's deserted?" he asked.

"Maybe."

"That's ridiculous."

"What's happened here is ridiculous." I stood. "I want to call more people in more places."

He got to his feet. "I don't think that's a good idea. Let's just get out of here. We can call people from Foster."

The word hit me like a sharp spike. "I'm not going back there!"

He was taken back by my reaction. "I didn't mean, Rox—"

"I know," I said quickly. Then I shrugged. "This is not my day. First I go for an abortion, and then I end up in the twilight zone." I pointed to Mike's Electron-ic Repair, next to Baskin-Robbins. "Look, let's make a couple of calls. Maybe we can reach someone who'll tell us what's happening."

Pepper hesitated. "Fine. But let's make it quick."

The door to Mike's shop was locked. Pepper paused for a second, glanced up and down the block, and then kicked in the glass beside the door. I jumped at the sound. Pepper reached inside and undid the latch.

"We'll have to tell Mike we did this," I said. I wanted to add, *"If we ever see him again."* We stepped inside. Mike had lived in Salem a hundred years and there was nothing he couldn't fix—radios, TVs, refrigerators—as long as they didn't have any microchips in them. Mike hated any silicon wonders. He called them microshits. His shop was simple, crammed with the internal organs of modern conveniences. An oil-stained phone sat on his cluttered workbench. Pepper picked it up.

"Who should we call first?" he asked.

"Information."

"Seriously?"

"I am serious," I said. "If they don't answer, call the operator."

He did as I requested. Information was not there. He tried the operator. The same thing. He slammed down the phone. "There must be something wrong with the lines," he said.

"Did you get a normal dial tone?" I asked.

"Yes, I got a normal dial tone."

I reached for the phone. "I want to call my grandmother in Portland. She hasn't left her house since I was born." I dialed the number from memory. It rang forever, although I kept praying for it to stop. But I couldn't take the phone away from my ear. Pepper finally had to put the receiver down. He was studying me as if he was worried I was about to lose my mind. He had every right to be concerned.

"Rox . . ." he began.

"There's no one there," I whispered. "The world's empty."

"Don't talk like that. There's been an evacuation of the area. The National Guard—"

"Screw the National Guard," I interrupted.

He grabbed me. "Your grandmother's probably still asleep. Call someone else."

"No."

"Do it, damn you! We're not alone!"

"Yes, we are," a voice said behind us.

41

IN WALKED STAN REESE. SHORT CHUBBY EIGHTEEN-YEAR-old Stan surprised me so bad I almost peed my pants. Child prodigy. Probable valedictorian of our class. Good old Stan. Ask him a question about math or science and if he didn't know the answer, there was none. His brown eyes were huge because his glasses were thick. He came in and sat on Mike's favorite stool. His pleasant plump face was a haven of sanity. He scratched at his dirty blond hair and sniffled.

"I hope I didn't scare you guys," he said calmly.

I let go of Pepper and moved to Stan, hugging him so tightly I could have hurt him. But Stan didn't complain. He wasn't only smart, he was cool. He was the rarest of intellectuals—he never acted superior. He smiled briefly as I let him go. He reset his glasses on his nose.

"It's too bad it took the end of the world for Roxanne to give me a hug," he said.

"I'm so glad to see you," I exclaimed, messing up his hair. I knew Stan fairly well. Our junior year I took algebra, and because I had the bad habit of ditching class every other day, the teacher assigned Stan to tutor me. Stan wasn't in my class, of course. He was already on his second semester of college calculus, but he was doing some kind of work-study project. I saw him twice a week for an hour, and in that time he taught me more than the teacher could have ever taught me. I ended up getting a B in the class, and taking Stan out for ice cream afterward to thank him. He really liked ice cream. He had a banana split *and* a malt. He had a rather major problem with his weight.

Pepper stepped forward. We had never talked about Stan, but I suspected Pepper hardly knew him. "What do you mean, the end of the world?" Pepper asked. "Has there been a nuclear war?"

"Not that I'm aware of," Stan said.

"Then what are you saying?" Pepper demanded.

"Everybody in the world seems to have disappeared," Stan replied.

"That's insane," Pepper sneered.

"Tell me about it," Stan said. He sat for a moment without speaking—we all did. When Stan spoke next, his voice was curiously intrigued, as if our situation were nothing but a fascinating scientific problem, which I suppose it was in a way. "I'm a short wave operator," he said. "Have been for years. I usually talk to three buddies of mine in Europe every Saturday morning. There's one each in France, Germany, and Switzerland. The one in France is a thirty-year-old woman, who's been teaching me French for the last six months. Well, to make a long story short, I tried to get in touch with them this morning. I couldn't get any of them. I checked out my equipment. It was perfect. I tried getting other people I talk to occasionally: a guy in Australia with chronic insomnia, a priest in India —these guys are almost always on the airways. I got zip. I began to scan all the bans. I was receiving fine. But nobody was transmitting. I turned on a normal radio, a TV."

"I did the same thing!" I exclaimed.

"What did you get?" Stan asked.

"Static," I said. "Fuzz."

Stan nodded. "That's what I got."

"I don't believe any of this," Pepper protested.

Stan pointed. "Turn on Mike's TV right there. That one's his—it's not in for repair."

Pepper did as he was told. He got a screen of fuzz, no matter how many times he flipped the channel. He snapped it off. "It proves nothing," he said, angry.

"It proves a lot," Stan said. "All the networks and local stations have suddenly stopped broadcasting."

"Why?" I asked.

"I don't why," Stan said.

"But you're Mr. Brain," Pepper said. "You get all the good grades. Use your brain now. Give us something."

Stan sighed. "My first reaction would be to say that there has been a major EMP high in the atmosphere. That's an electromagnetic pulse. A multiple megaton warhead detonated at say, forty miles altitude, could knock out all our electronics."

"Then we are at war," I moaned.

"Not that I know of," Stan repeated. "An EMP

would have killed this TV here. And my short wave, and your radio. We wouldn't be getting fuzz, we'd be getting nothing. Plus an EMP wouldn't explain the disappearance of everybody."

"Then give us another explanation," Pepper said. "What about a toxic spill or something like that?"

Stan spread his hands. "I got up this morning, and after realizing that there was no one on my radio or TV, I went to my parents' bedroom. There was no one in their bed. There was no one in the house. If my parents had been evacuated in the middle of the night, don't you think they'd at least awaken me? Ask me if I wanted to come?"

"Was their bed messed up?" I asked.

Stan nodded. "Good question. Yes, it was unmade. My mother never left a bed unmade more than ten minutes in her whole life. I think they were in bed when they left."

"When they left where?" Pepper asked.

"I don't know," Stan repeated.

I felt faint and couldn't think clearly. All the rules had been changed. Reality had fallen asleep at the wheel and driven off the road. I had to sit down. Pepper pounded his leg in frustration.

"We can't just sit here," he said. "We have to find out what's happened. I say we get a car and drive to another town."

"We might have to do that eventually," Stan said. "But I wouldn't start our investigation by traveling."

"Why not?" Pepper asked.

"What's in another town that's not here?" Stan

asked. "More people? Maybe, maybe not. But we already know for a fact that most of the people on earth are gone. I can tell if a radio or a TV's been damaged. There was nothing wrong with mine. I doubt there was anything wrong with Roxanne's. That means that no one, in any part of the world, is transmitting. And that means this effect is not localized to here."

"But we have to find more people," Pepper protested.

"We may find more people in Salem itself," Stan said. "We should look here first. People freak out when the unexpected happens. What's happened today is about as unexpected as you can get. If we go driving from town to town, we might end up getting shot at by someone."

Pepper considered. He always had strong opinions, but logic worked wonders on him, and everything Stan had said made sense. "All right," Pepper said finally. "We'll stay here for now. But what do we do here?"

Stan paced in front of us. "If there are other people in town, what would they do first? Once they discovered what had happened?"

"They'd probably go through all the steps we have," I said. "Then they'd leave town."

"What would they do just before they left town?" Stan asked.

"Steal a good car and a sack full of cash," Pepper said.

"Ah." Stan raised an approving finger. He had

probably known the answer before asking for our input. "We all want easy money. What a time to get it."

"Let's go to the bank," I said.

"Right," Stan said, agreeing with me.

"Let's go," Pepper said, anxious to do something, anything.

There were two banks in Salem, on opposite corners of the town square. We went to the small one first—a First Interstate. Our break-in tactics had lost their subtlety already. Pepper simply kicked the door in. We looked around, called out. No one.

The next bank—a Security Pacific—was Salem's main center of commerce. I had been in it only a couple of days earlier, when I had withdrawn my half of the abortion money. The teller had asked if I was going to use the cash for a present or for a vacation weekend. I had said, "Yeah, right, both." Give me the cash and mind your own business. It was a big bank, no doubt full of big bucks. As we approached, we could see the front door had already been smashed in, which made us hurry toward it. Stan stopped us before we could enter, though.

"Whoever was here has probably already come and gone," Stan said. "But maybe we should call out before we enter. We don't want to surprise anybody."

"Good idea," Pepper said. He stuck his face close to the hole in the front door. "Hello!" he called. He got no response. "We must have missed them," he muttered, pulling the door open.

A glass panel beside the door suddenly shattered into lethal-looking shards. A loud roar accompanied the display. Instinctively we threw ourselves to the sides of the door, pressing against the brick walls. I was alone on my side, the left side.

"You should have yelled louder," Stan told Pepper.

"Or not yelled at all," Pepper grumbled. "Are you all right, Rox?"

"Yeah," I gasped. "But maybe we should stop by the bank later." A warm, sticky sensation on my right leg got my attention. I looked down and was amazed to see a dark stain growing through my blue jeans. "I've been shot," I whispered.

"We've got to get out of here," Stan said, seeing my wound.

"That sonofabitch," Pepper swore. "Can you walk, Rox?"

Gingerly I probed my wound. I had never been shot before. I wanted to be cool like the characters on TV and just rip off a piece of my shirt and bandage my wound on the spot. But I felt suddenly nauseous. I had to brace myself against the wall just to keep from falling over.

"I think I've just been grazed," I managed to get out. "I don't think there's a bullet in my leg."

"I'm going over to her," Pepper said to Stan.

"Be quick," Stan advised.

Pepper leapt across the distance between us. It was a good thing. A second and third shot disintegrated what was left of the glass. Pepper put a supporting arm around me.

"I'll carry you," he said.

I brushed him off. "No, I can walk. Let's just get out of here."

"I'm getting a rifle and coming back and wasting this guy," Pepper hissed. He grabbed my hand and nodded in the direction of some buildings out of the line of sight of the ruined bank doors. "Let's do it."

We were just preparing to launch our getaway, when a voice called out from inside the bank. "Who's there?" it said.

Pepper was enraged. "Who's there?" he screamed. "We're here! Who are you? And why are you shooting at us?"

There was a long pause. "Is that you, Pepper?"

"Yeah!" Pepper yelled back. "Who are you?"

"It's Helter."

Helter Skater, better known as Helter Skelter, wanted to be a bad dude. He wanted it so bad, and took on so many of the trappings of toughness, that he had ended up as a topic of light gossip. He smoked, he drank, he had tattoos—all the basics. But he also committed at least one significant act of violence a month. He did it with such regularity it was as if he marked it off on a calendar beforehand. In March he got in an argument with the football quarterback at school and ended up breaking the guy's jaw. He was suspended for the act, but only for a couple of days because the quarterback had thrown more interceptions than touchdowns the previous seasons. In April Helter got in a fight with a biker at a local bar. It was true the biker had seen better days in the nineteen-fifties and was alone and very drunk, but the way Helter told the story he had taken on a gang of Hell's

Angels with only his fists to defend himself. Now it was a May stardate and he had just shot Roxanne Wells in the leg.

"Are you done shooting at us?" Pepper called out, furious. Helter was bigger than my boyfriend, and obviously more practiced at the violent arts, but I suspected if push came to shove Pepper would have torn Helter's head off.

"Yeah, you can come in," Helter called.

"I'm coming in, all right," Pepper said and kicked the door open. Stan and I chased after him. I was still bleeding, but it was going to have to wait. If there were only four people left alive on the planet, it wasn't going to do for one to get killed.

"Pepper," I called after him. "Don't start anything."

"I don't have to start it," he snapped. "You're bleeding. That's a hell of a start, already. Where are you, you yellow bastard?"

Helter was, of course, back beside the vault, where all the money was kept. He had obviously blown the lock off the vault because his black windbreaker pockets were fat with hundreds, and his pants pockets bulged with rolled green wads. He carried a mean rifle in his left hand, and I believe it was still smoking. He did not point it at Pepper as my boyfriend strode up, but he shook it a little. Tucked in his belt was a Colt .45 revolver.

"Don't mess with me, Pepper," he said. "I didn't know who it was out there."

"You just decided when you woke up this morning

that you would shoot at anything that moved, huh?"
Pepper demanded, momentarily halting his advance.

"If I wanted to hit you," Helter snapped back,
"you'd be dead."

I raised my hand. "Excuse me, my leg is bleeding.
How come I'm not dead?"

"Oh," Helter mumbled, chagrined. I could never
decide whether he was attractive in a crude way, or
just plain ugly. His hair was blond, plowed down to
the roots, and his deeply tanned face was surprisingly
featureless. He had two expressions: anger or vague
confusion. I suppose he could look frightened, too,
but I hadn't been around him all that much. He was a
senior like the rest of us, but he moved in different
circles.

"I should kick in your face," Pepper said.

Helter put his attitude back on. "What's stopping
you?"

"I think it's the fact that you're holding two deadly
weapons," Stan observed.

Helter scowled. "What are you doing here?"

"Closing out my account," Stan replied. Then he
did a very brave thing. He stepped forward and
plucked the rifle out of Helter's hand. He didn't touch
the revolver, however. Helter was so amazed he didn't
even try to stop him. Stan set the rifle on a nearby seat,
adding, "Let's kiss and make up and get down to
business. All right guys?"

"It's all right with me," Helter said, trying to act
bored.

"Just our luck he should have been left," Pepper

muttered. He turned to me. "I want to look at your leg. Are you in pain?"

I nodded to all the money in the area. "Yeah. But I feel a lot better knowing that we're rich."

Pepper had me sit and felt my cut. He decided that the bullet had just grazed me. He ripped off a part of his shirt and tied it tightly over the wound. The bleeding began to slow immediately.

"Are you strong enough to walk to the drugstore?" Pepper asked.

"Sure," I said. "It's only next door."

"I can give you a piggyback ride," Helter offered, guilty at last.

"No thanks," I said politely. I wasn't really that mad at him.

"Could I have a piggyback ride?" Stan asked Helter hopefully.

"What a group," Helter growled.

At the drugstore Pepper made the other two stay up front at the cash register while I sat down in the back beside the prescription drugs. I slipped down my pants so he could clean and bandage my wound. It was kind of romantic.

"They do this in westerns all the time," I said as he taped the gauze to my thigh. I could tell he was enjoying the sight of my legs; they were good ones.

"I don't remember any drugstores in westerns," he said.

"That's true." I reached down and held his hands. His eyes met mine. If I was looking for strength, it was there for the taking. The only thing that made our situation bearable was that we were together. "What are we going to do?" I asked.

"First we have to figure out what's happened and then I guess we'll do the right thing." He glanced in the direction of the others. "We're lucky we have Stan with us. The guy's sharp."

"You like him, I'm glad. He really is a wonderful person. But be nice to Helter as well. We'll get nowhere if we're at one another's throats."

"I'll tolerate him. I will not be nice to him."

Pepper finished with my leg and we rejoined the others. We hardly had a chance to catch up on Helter's story, and his ours, when blond, beautiful Leslie Belle strolled through the door. Her eyes were dry but both her cheeks were streaked. She had on bright blue pajamas and no shoes.

"I have a splitting headache," she said flatly. "Any of you guys got an aspirin?"

CHAPTER V

LESLIE BELLE WAS BEAUTY AND SUCCESS. SHE GOT GOOD grades, starred in practically every play at Salem High—and she glowed. She was the kind of girl that girls like myself were supposed to despise. And yet, though I knew her well enough to know her faults, I had never been able to dislike her. I believed she deserved her popularity. Her looks could not be denied. Her blue eyes were brilliant by day, and sparkled at night. She had bones and teeth that spelled sun and fun, and a body that made most guys think party time.

But she wasn't loose, at least not from what I'd heard, and even more remarkable, she wasn't a snob. Once when I sprained my ankle, and had to hobble around on crutches, she carried my books to and from the classes we shared. And she performed the service without making me feel self-conscious. Of course, she wasn't perfect. She had a tendency to talk about herself. She did so quite innocently, as if she honestly believed Leslie Belle was what you did want to hear about. The odd thing was, she was usually right. She

54

led a much more exciting life than the average Salem High girl.

Now, though, she didn't look too excited or exciting. Stan fetched her a bottle of Tylenol and a can of Coke from the drugstore cooler. She swallowed three of the pills in one gulp, and then leaned against the counter, staring blankly at a row of diapers.

"Does somebody want to talk or should I just start screaming?" she said finally.

"Nice pajamas," Helter said.

"Thanks," Leslie mumbled.

"Have you seen anybody else beside us?" I asked.

"Nope," Leslie said. "Is there anybody else?"

"We're not sure," Stan said.

Leslie nodded slowly. Then her beautiful face began to fall to pieces. Her lower lip quivered. Her cheeks trembled and the tears fell. Pepper was by her side in a moment, his comforting arms around her. That was OK, I suppose, though I would have been happy to comfort her myself.

"Shh," Pepper crooned. "It's not so bad. We'll be all right. Don't cry." He drew out a handkerchief. He had never offered me one before. "Here, blow your nose. You'll feel better."

"I just can't find anybody," Leslie moaned in his chest.

"What a fox," Helter whispered to Stan, shaking his head.

"Let's go get some ice cream," Stan said. "I think better when I'm eating."

* * *

We broke into Baskin-Robbins. Pepper let Helter kick in the door, much to Helter's pleasure. Stan's tastes were simple, though immense. He plucked a five-gallon tub of chocolate chip out of the freezer chest, grabbed a spoon, and got to work. Helter didn't even bother with a spoon, the barbarian. Leslie wasn't hungry. Pepper and I shared a cup of vanilla. The situation was hilarious. The world had ended and there we were eating ice cream.

"Should we have our big talk now or should we go looking for more people first?" Stan asked, looking quite happy to sit there and finish the tub.

"I don't want to talk," Helter said. "I want to get out of here."

"And where do you want to go?" Stan asked.

"Los Angeles," Helter said without hesitation. He had returned to the bank for his rifle and was keeping it close, along with his revolver, which he had set on the table beside his ice cream.

"Why there?" I asked.

Helter shrugged. "I've always wanted to go there."

Pepper snorted. "So have I, but the situation's changed a bit, don't you think?"

Helter was not impressed. "L.A.'s a big city. There'll be more survivors there."

"More survivors of what?" Pepper asked.

"Of whatever's happened," Helter said simply.

"And what has happened?" Pepper asked him.

"I don't know," Helter said. "Isn't that what Stan wants to talk about?"

"We do need to talk," Stan said diplomatically.

"Leslie, are you sure you don't want any ice cream? You can have your choice of thirty-one flavors."

"I'd rather not," she replied, clutching Pepper's handkerchief to her chest. Her gaze was far off. I believed she was in shock, and knew that Stan believed the same thing about her. He set aside his spoon and reached out to touch her hands.

"Why don't you tell us what happened to you this morning?" he asked.

She stared at him a moment. "Nothing happened."

"Tell us," Stan insisted gently.

Leslie gestured helplessly. "I woke up and my parents were out. I couldn't understand why they would suddenly leave without telling me or leaving me a note. I made myself breakfast. I had a bowl of corn flakes and strawberries. Then I turned on the radio, but it was broken. I called a couple of my girlfriends, but no one answered. Then I started to get scared."

"You felt like you were surrounded by emptiness?" I said.

Leslie nodded. "I feel that way still, even with you guys here. I stepped outside on our porch. There were no cars on the road, no people. I began to walk up the street. At first I called out, but no one answered. Then I just walked without saying anything. I walked for a long time."

"You must have been happy to see us," Helter said gamely.

Leslie remained solemn. "I don't even know if you guys are real. Why should I be happy?"

"We're real," Pepper said. He, too, reached over

and squeezed her hands. It seemed the in thing to do. No one had squeezed mine in the last half hour, and I had got shot.

"About what time did you wake up, Leslie?" Stan asked.

"I don't know. The sun was up."

Stan nodded. "Helter, tell us your tale."

"Mine's like hers, except I didn't get all freaked out," Helter said. "I woke up and realized everybody had split. I figured I'd split, too. I got a gun, I was getting some bread. I was heading for the Coast. Then you guys showed up."

"And you decided to shoot us," Pepper said bitterly.

"You startled me, all right?" Helter said. "I told you I was sorry."

"You never said you were sorry," I said.

"Well, so what?" Helter said. "Who has time to be sorry with all this weird crap going on?"

"What time did you get up?" Stan asked Helter.

"A little after eight," Helter said.

"You guys said you were out of town this morning when this change happened," Stan said to me and Pepper. "Give me more details. Where exactly were you?"

"We started off in Foster," Pepper said.

"What were you doing there?" Stan asked.

"We were visiting friends," I said quickly.

"What time did you leave Foster?" Stan asked.

Pepper glanced at me. "About six," I said.

"Were your friends up when you left?" Stan asked.

"Yes," I said, thinking of the doctor and nasty nurse.

"You saw them?" Stan asked. "You talked to them?"

"Sure, they were awake," I said. "Why?"

"Have you tried calling them since you left Foster?" Stan asked.

"No," I said.

"Do you want to try?" Stan asked.

"No," I said. "I mean, I know they won't be home. They told us they were going out."

Stan paused. He was sharp. I could tell he suspected I was hiding something. "What did you do after you left Foster?" he asked.

"We drove straight here," I said.

"Who drove?" Stan asked.

"I did."

"What did you do, Pepper?" Stan asked.

"Nothing. Dozed off."

Stan was interested. "Did you sleep the whole way back?"

"No," Pepper said. "I woke up when we got to that gas station out on Thirty-seven. You know the one?"

"Yeah," Stan said. "What time was that?"

"Close to eight," Pepper said. "There was no one at the station. We thought it had been robbed."

"And from there you drove straight into town?" Stan asked.

"Yeah," Pepper said. "What are you getting at?"

"I'm trying to find a common denominator," Stan said. "Roxanne, was the sun up when you left Foster?"

"No. But there was light in the east."

"Did you see anyone while driving back?" Stan asked.

"No," I said, then paused. "Wait a second. There was a hitchhiker. I saw her way ahead of me on the road. She was standing in the glare of the rising sun. But when I got to where she was, she was gone."

"What do you mean?" Stan asked. "Did she dash off the road?"

"I suppose. Like I said, I had the sun in my eyes. I just blinked and she was gone. It's funny—at the time I thought I might have imagined her. But I remember her hair. It was long and red, bright red in fact. And she was wearing a long black coat."

"Where was this?" Stan asked.

"In the middle of the desert," I said. "Halfway between here and Foster."

"Did she look like anybody you knew?" Stan asked.

"No," I said.

"This is interesting," Stan said.

"What?" Pepper asked.

"Several things," Stan said. "Roxanne was the only one who was awake when the change occurred. The rest of us were all asleep."

"So?" I said. "That could just be coincidence."

"Maybe," Stan said. "But let me point out something else that can't be coincidence. Look at the five of us here. What do you see?"

"Do we have to include Helter in this question?" Pepper asked.

"You just watch your mouth," Helter growled.

"We're all about the same age," I said, stunned that I hadn't seen the truth earlier. "We all go to school together."

"Exactly," Stan said. "Why? Why is it that the only five people left in town happen to know each other? What do we have in common?"

"I don't get it," Pepper interrupted. "Who cares? I want to know where everyone's gone. That's the question we should be asking."

Stan shook his head. "What if everybody's gone nowhere?"

"Huh?" Helter said.

"Naturally we assume something has happened to everybody else," Stan said. "But what if we have it backward. What if something's happened to us?"

There was a moment of silence—a profoundly deep silence that could not normally be found on the planet earth. The only sound was a low whistling of the wind that we could hear through the open door. Raising my eyes to the sky I noticed something else.

"There are no birds," I said.

"Who cares about the birds?" Helter asked.

"No, it's true," Pepper said, staring out through the plate-glass window of the ice-cream parlor. "I haven't seen a bird since I woke up at the gas station."

Stan nodded grimly. "I haven't seen any dogs or cats or even bugs. I suspect if we took a sample of our skin, we wouldn't find any bacteria."

Helter looked disgusted. "I would sure as hell hope not."

"My point is that *all* living things have vanished,"

Stan said. "Except for us, and perhaps a few more people in town. But to tell you the truth, I'm not sure if anyone's vanished—except us."

"Are you saying that we're no longer on earth?" Pepper asked. "That we've been picked up by a flying saucer?"

"Maybe," Stan said.

Pepper snorted. "That's the most idiotic suggestion I ever heard. I'm surprised at you, Stan."

"Since we are in an impossible situation," Stan said, not taking offense, "we must be open to all possibilities. How many of you have heard of the Bermuda Triangle?"

"Are those those new bikinis that show off a girl's butt?" Helter asked.

I patted Helter's hand. "I don't think you got that one right."

"It's an area in the ocean near Bermuda where a lot of planes and boats have disappeared," Pepper said.

"Yes," Stan said. "Until yesterday I would have said the Bermuda Triangle was impossible. But now I'm not sure. What kind of world are we in right now? An empty one? Its emptiness is selective then. There are no people or animals or insects, but there is food. There's electricity. This last point is interesting. Who's running the power stations?"

"Maybe no one," I said. "Maybe the power's just on for now, and it will fail later." I shuddered at the thought. Because now it was day. The sun was out and we were together. But come night, it could be very dark, and silent. It was strange how the silence preyed on my mind more than the emptiness. They weren't the same, I knew, not at all.

"That's possible," Stan said. "But my point is we appear to be in the same world we've always been in, but with a few important differences." He paused. "I wonder if we haven't fallen into our own Bermuda Triangle."

"You mean, like into another dimension?" I asked.

"Yes," Stan said.

"What does 'another dimension' mean?" Helter wanted to know.

"In a sense, nothing," Stan said. "You don't understand something just because you give it a name. But I think it's worth talking this way because I can tell you right now that we're not going to find a logical explanation for our predicament. Everyone in the world simply does not disappear overnight."

"You're depressing me," Helter complained.

"Then let me give you some encouragement," Stan said. "If we've fallen into another dimension, and we can figure out how, we might be able to climb back out."

"Hold on a second," Pepper said. "I'm not ready to accept this other dimension theory until we've looked at others."

"Go ahead," Stan said.

"I don't know any others!" Pepper said. "You suggest some."

"Flying saucers could have swooped in during the night and beamed everyone aboard except us," Stan said.

"Be serious," Pepper said.

"I am being serious," Stan said. "You're not accepting the fact that this phenomenon is worldwide. That being the case, all our theories will have to be ridiculous."

"Could we just be dreaming?" I asked.

"This is no normal dream," Stan said carefully, considering the idea. "I certainly feel like I'm awake. Then again, dreaming people often do."

"We must be dreaming," Leslie whispered, and there was suddenly hope in her voice. She sat up in her chair and there was color in her cheeks. Yet I couldn't say I preferred her wide-eyed look to the flat one of a moment ago. "We can just wake ourselves up!" she exclaimed.

"Leslie," I said.

"No, Rox," she said, jumping to her feet. "It makes sense. We'll all pinch ourselves and we'll wake up in bed." Her voice cracked as she laughed. "We won't have to worry about aliens and space ships. We'll just roll over and turn off the alarm."

"We could try that, Leslie, if you want," Stan said, obviously concerned. "But I don't want you to get upset if it doesn't work. We have to be—"

"It will work!" she interrupted. "But we have to do it together. Come on, you guys, let's get ready to pinch our arms on the count of three. One—"

"I wouldn't mind pinching other things," Helter muttered to Pepper.

"Two—"

"Leslie," I began again.

"Three!" Leslie cried, pinching her arm. "Pinch,

pinch, pinch, everyone. Harder. Faster. You're not doing it hard enough!"

The four of us watched as Leslie hacked at her arm for perhaps twenty seconds. Then Pepper stood and held her—my, that was twice in a row—and helped her back into her seat. Once there she burst into sobs and had to be comforted by another of Pepper's strong hugs. I don't mean to sound unsympathetic. Leslie was hurting—there was no doubt of that—but he was my boyfriend. I wished Helter would comfort her. Of course Helter would probably have tried to get in a feel in the process.

"This has got to be a dream," Leslie cried.

"Leslie," Stan said patiently with great strength in his voice. "You have to relax. The situation is strange, but we're not in any danger. We're together, and together we can solve this puzzle and make things right."

Leslie stared at him with a combination of hope and disbelief. "How do you know we're not in danger?" she whispered, sniffing.

"Because if there's nothing, nothing can hurt us," Stan said. He considered a moment. "I keep thinking about Roxanne's story. The change—I don't know what else to call it—appears to have occurred around sunrise. And except for Roxanne, none of us was awake at sunrise." He paused again. "Except for the hitchhiker."

"I'm not even sure she was there," I said.

"But you were able to describe her," Stan said. "You must have seen her. Are there any other details you remember?"

I hesitated. "No."

"Are you sure?" Stan asked.

I frowned. "I was just thinking how when I saw her she looked like a shadow across the sun. It came up exactly behind where she stood."

"Another coincidence," Stan said.

"Stan," Pepper complained. "You're sounding superstitious."

Stan grinned. "An empty planet could do that to the most hardened scientist." His grin faded. "She was wearing a black coat," he muttered to himself.

"I'm not sure what she had on," I said.

Stan looked at me sharply. "Her hair was long and red, bright red you said. Isn't that odd?"

"I have red hair," I said, not understanding where he was coming from.

"Yes, but yours isn't bright red," Stan said. He thought a moment. "She reminds me of someone. Do any of you know who?"

"No," Pepper and Helter replied together. They turned to each other, surprised. Leslie suddenly sat up but didn't say anything.

"Who?" I asked.

"Betty Sue McCormick," Stan said.

"Why do you bring her up?" Pepper asked impatiently.

"She was just a suicidal weirdo," Helter said.

"And she's dead. She's been dead four weeks," Leslie added, and the words sent a shiver through the length of my body. Because the more I thought back to the hitchhiker, the more it seemed possible it had been Betty Sue. That hair—it was as if her head had caught on fire from the rising sun. And then she had vanished, like the last traces of night at dawn.

Of course, it couldn't have been her. No way, José, I thought.

"She died in a raging fire," Stan said. "I heard there were hardly any of her teeth left to identify her by."

The four of us were incredulous. "Are you saying she's alive?" Pepper asked angrily. Stan raised an eyebrow at his reaction.

"What's the big deal?" Stan asked.

"That's what we're asking you," Helter said.

"Betty Sue is dead," Leslie said solemnly. "Let's not talk about her."

"Yeah," Pepper said. "We're just getting off on tangents."

"She was just a bitch," Helter added.

Stan's eyes narrowed on Helter. Stan wore thick glasses and was short, but he was no lightweight—that was clear. "She wasn't a bitch," he said. "She was my friend."

"I was just talking," Helter mumbled.

"She was an unusual girl, though," Pepper said.

"That's for sure," Leslie whispered.

Stan turned his attention to Leslie. "You knew her the best. You grew up practically next door to her."

"So what?" Leslie snapped. "I told you, I don't want to talk about her."

"Why not?" Stan asked. And he stopped her before she could reply. "Why are all of you fidgeting in your seats at the mention of Betty Sue's name?"

"I'm not," I said. "I hardly knew her."

"But the rest of you knew her, judging by your

reactions," Stan said. "Come on, let's speak our minds. What's the big deal?"

"Stan," Pepper said, "we're in a big mess here, and you're the only one of us who has a big brain. We want you to help us get out of this mess. We don't want to talk about a girl who killed herself four weeks ago." I couldn't help but notice the uneasiness in his voice.

"Absolutely," Helter said.

"I agree," Leslie put in.

Stan was stoic. "What if I want to talk about her?"

"But why?" Pepper cried. Once more, his reaction was startling to me. Pepper had never mentioned Betty Sue—not even at the time of her death. Never once. He looked over at me and sat back in his seat. "This is silly," he muttered.

Stan studied him a moment then sighed. He leaned toward me. "Roxanne," he said. "Could it have been Betty Sue on the road?"

"No," I said. "She's dead."

"What if she wasn't dead?" Stan said. "What if she faked her death? What if she did that to throw everybody off, and then left town for the past month?"

"And waited out in the middle of the desert until today?" I asked, more confused by the second. "Until I drove by?"

"If you like," Stan said. "Could it have been her on the road?"

I hesitated. "It's possible."

"We have to stop this," Leslie said, and there was a note of desperation in her voice. "Betty Sue was nothing!"

"She was someone," Stan said quietly. He lowered

his head and seemed to be thinking a moment. When he raised it back up, his expression was dark. "I liked her." He cleared his throat. "How many of you liked her?" No one responded. "How many of you hated her?"

"None of us hated her," Pepper said impatiently.

"I hated her," Helter said.

"Why?" Stan asked.

"I told you, she was a bitch," Helter said. "At least to me."

"She wasn't bitchy to me," said Leslie. "But she was a spooky girl."

"What made her spooky?" I asked, curious. Leslie was coming out of her shock. The mention of Betty Sue had done it. She was still afraid, but now she had fight in her, too.

She leveled her gaze at me. "Just take my word for it," she said.

"Stan," Pepper said. "I am going to ask you one last time. Why do you want to talk about her?"

Stan shrugged. "I don't know. I just have this feeling. . . . Maybe she's the common denominator in this situation."

"In what possible way?" Pepper asked, exasperated.

"We all knew her," Stan said.

"We all knew lots of people," Pepper protested. "We all went to the same school for Christsakes. Besides, Rox hardly knew her."

"But Roxanne is the one who might have seen her on the road," Stan said.

"She doesn't know if she saw anybody," Pepper said.

"I saw somebody," I whispered. Yet the words rang false in my ears. I had wanted to say I saw *something*. A shadow. A ghost. Stan was right—just the mention of Betty Sue's name had thrown the others.

Pepper had given up. "What do you want to do with Betty Sue?" he asked Stan.

"I don't want to *do* anything with her," Stan said. "But I'd like to find her, if she's alive and in this neighborhood."

"I want to find other people first," Leslie interrupted. "I want to drive around town with our horns blaring."

"Why don't we just shoot off guns in the square?" Helter asked. He was itching to play soldier.

"Because if people are still here, they'll run the other way," Pepper said. "I say we follow Leslie's suggestion. At least it's something to do."

"And if we do this, and we don't find anyone else," Stan said, "then can we look for Betty Sue?"

"Where would we look?" I asked. "The desert?"

Stan glanced out the window. The wind continued to blow, and it appeared to be picking up. The town had been immaculate when we had returned that morning, but already the square was covered with a faint coating of sand. It was easy to imagine how, if no one returned to wipe it away, the town would slowly be buried.

"No," Stan said. "We'll stay out of the desert for now. We'll go to her house. We'll see what's there."

It was then I realized Stan was keeping something from us, as Pepper and I had kept something from him. I hoped it was nothing bad.

CHAPTER VI

WE DROVE AROUND TOWN FOR AN HOUR IN A CAR WE borrowed with the horn blaring. We talked little while we went up and down the streets. The sand bristled against the windshield the whole time. We found no one and no one found us. The odd thing was—none of us was surprised. It was like the gang had been assembled and that was that. Finally I glanced over at Stan, who sat in the backseat between Helter and Leslie.

"I don't know where she lived," I said.

"Two thirty-two Chesterfield," Stan said. "Take Magnolia away from the square and turn right. You'll see it halfway down on the right, behind a white picket fence and a hedge of rose bushes."

"A hedge of thorns," Leslie muttered, putting her hand to her head as if she was in pain.

"Why do you say that?" Stan asked.

"I'm not saying anything," Leslie replied.

We arrived at the house five minutes later. I had never been there before, but the others climbed out of the car with what could best be described as expressions of dread. Even Stan. I kept wanting to ask

Pepper how he knew Betty Sue, but didn't want to do it until we were alone. One thing for sure—there was no way he was telling me he hadn't known her. And pretty good from what I could see.

"Maybe I should stay outside and stand guard," Helter said, shouldering his rifle.

"What's the matter?" Pepper asked. "Are you afraid?"

"I'm not afraid of an empty house," Helter replied, kicking at a wooden post on the white picket fence. The house was much the same as the surrounding homes: small and boxlike, with a tired green tar tiled roof and a white paint job that was cracking from having stared too long at the sun. Yet the house seemed to be in shadow, and instinctively I raised my eyes to find the tree that shaded it. But there was no tree, no shadow. It must have been my imagination, I thought. Suddenly I wasn't crazy about going into that house either.

"I'm not going in," Leslie said.

"You want to stay out here with Helter?" Stan asked.

Helter grinned at Leslie. A troll with acne would have looked more appealing. "I'll take care of you, babe," he promised.

"I think we should stick together," Pepper said, and I hoped it wasn't because he didn't want Leslie and Helter alone together.

"That's all right with me," Stan said. "If we can get everyone inside."

"I'm not afraid," Helter said again, his hand drifting to the revolver tucked in his belt. He wiped the sweat off his forehead with the back of his hand. The day was hot, and that felt real enough.

"I can't stay out here by myself," Leslie complained.

"You probably went into this house a million times while you were growing up," Stan said to Leslie. She lowered her head.

"But I haven't been inside in years," she said.

"Where do you live?" I asked.

Leslie pointed to a house a couple of houses over. "There."

"And it's been years?" I asked. "Did you have a falling out?"

Leslie nodded weakly. "You could call it that."

"Are we going in or not?" Pepper asked. "And what are we looking for when we get inside?"

"Evidence," Stan said, leading the way.

The front door was unlocked. Stan knocked nevertheless, and then even waited for a moment before stepping inside. "Hello?" he said. We crowded behind him. The word floated out and died. We all took another step forward and tried not to breathe. The place was musty. The furniture could have been cut out of a textbook depicting the values of lower-class middle America. The beige wallpaper was a discount buy, and the glue that had been used to hang it had been lumpy. Cheap copies of Biblical paintings covered the walls. We looked at them in wonder because in every one of them either Jesus, an apostle, or some saint was bleeding.

"Her mother's a religious fanatic," Leslie said flatly.

"I know," Stan said, and the way he said it—he knew even more. He pointed down the hall. "Let's go into her room."

We moved as a group, bumping into one another, afraid of the skeletons we would surely find in her closet. Betty Sue's room was obviously a reaction against her mother. Here there were no disturbing paintings of pierced and bleeding saints. No motel beige. This room was stark ultra modern, painted in shades of gray and white. A neat wooden desk sat beneath the sole window. On top of it was a closed book, like a diary, and a sheaf of loose notebook pages, held in place by the book. The window was open part way and the pages ruffled in the breeze.

"I haven't been here in a while either," Stan said softly.

"When was the last time?" I asked.

"Four weeks ago. The day she died," Stan said.

"You saw her that day?" I asked. "How was she?" Stan met my gaze. "Happy."

"Well, we're here. Now can we go?" Pepper said.

"What's the hurry?" I asked.

"What's the point in staying?" he asked coolly.

"I want to look at her papers," Stan said. He stepped up to the desk. We crowded in behind him. He picked up what looked like the diary and confirmed that it was indeed Betty Sue's secret jottings. Yet I wondered if that was true—how secret they were, I mean. It was almost as if the book and pages had been left there for someone to find. Stan ignored the loose pages for a moment and flipped open the diary at random. We read over his shoulder.

Dear Diary,
Today we had a party for Leslie. She was ten. I am ten. Now we're both ten. We sang and played games. Her mom brought out a cake with ten candles. We told her to make a wish and she did. But she wouldn't tell anybody what it was because she said it wouldn't come true. But she smiled at me as she said it. She knew she'd tell me. And that Fat Freddy would make it come true. He always does.

I think I will go to sleep now and dream about Mars. I haven't been there in a long time.

"Who the hell is Fat Freddy?" Helter growled.
Stan looked at Leslie. "Do you know?"
Leslie shook her head slightly, obviously scared. She had turned the color of the gray carpet. "No," she whispered.
"You don't remember?" Stan asked.
"No," Leslie said, and we all knew she was lying. Stan flipped to another page, a later date.

Dear Diary,
Boys are beginning to look good. I like their mouths and their legs. Mom says that's what happens when a girl gets older—she likes to look at boys. But Mom says that boys aren't ever as nice as they look. In fact, she says most boys are

bad. I wonder if that's true. I don't think Sam Douglas is bad. He talks to me in math and always calls me by my full name. I hate when people just call me Betty. Steve Kinder always did that to annoy me. But Steve has moved away and I think he died. I hope so.

I would like to make Sam kiss me. I wonder if he would if I made him.

"Who the hell was Steve Kinder?" Helter asked.

"He moved away to Colorado when we were twelve," Stan said. "I used to know him pretty good."

"Do you know how he's doing?" I asked.

"He's dead," Stan said. "He got cancer right after leaving here." Stan turned to Leslie. "Did you know him?"

"I knew him" was all Leslie would say.

Stan turned forward a few more pages, and we read some more.

Dear Diary,

I am not happy with Leslie. I have done so much for her. I made her what she is. But now she is kissing Sam, and I am only writing words. I want to write harsh words about her. I know she would feel them. I might do that. I might make her feel like her lips were bleeding whenever she thought of kissing the boy I wanted to kiss. She had better be nice to me.

I dreamed of a rat last night. It was eating a dead man's hand. I think the man was dead. It would have hurt if he wasn't. I think he lived in

England. There's lots of fog there. I like the fog, although I've never seen it.

"Who was Sam?" Helter asked.

"My first boyfriend," Leslie mumbled, a vacant look in her eyes.

"What happened to him?" I asked.

"I'm not sure," Leslie said. "He moved away, too."

"What makes you think anything happened to him?" Pepper asked.

"It usually did," Leslie said.

Stan turned to another page. Betty Sue was growing up before our eyes. Into something most unusual.

Dear Diary,

I think dark thoughts and feel warm. I write in the unlighted chamber of my existence. I turn as I walk alone, and I imagine I see Fat Freddy following me. But he left when I changed into a young woman and dreamed of sin. He was too fat for my tastes and I had him for supper because he thought he was bigger than the god who created him.

I'm going to bed now. I'm going to dream now. I'm still hungry.

"We should stop," Leslie moaned.

"Why?" Stan demanded.

There were tears in Leslie's eyes and she was trembling. "It won't get any better," she whispered.

But Stan turned another few pages, and I saw a name that I did not want to see.

Dear Diary,

Helter took me for a ride in his car tonight. He yelled at a boy on a bike that got in our way and almost killed him. Helter would have killed him if I had let him. Maybe I shouldn't have been so concerned. Helter would look nice in striped pajamas and the shadow of metal bars. I am growing tired of Helter. But he thinks something wicked for me, and I want to see what it is. I am curious. I will imagine this a little further.

Pepper called me tonight. He has a nicer mouth than Helter and his nails are clean. I think he wants to kiss me. I think I will let him.

Pepper snapped the diary from Stan's hands. "I've had enough," Pepper said. "We're not going to read any more. This girl is dead for Godsakes. Let's just leave her alone."

I held out my hand. "I want to read some more."

"No," Pepper said, clasping the diary to his chest.

"He's right, let's just get out of here," Leslie said, and she sounded close to hysterics.

"Did you kiss her?" I demanded of my boyfriend.

"No," Pepper said. "I only went out with her once."

"When?" I asked.

"A long time ago," he said, and I think he was lying. "It was nothing."

"What about you?" Stan asked Helter.

"I only went out with her once too," Helter said quickly, and he was scared as well.

"It says in her diary you went out several times," I said.

"It doesn't say that," Helter said.

"It implies it," I said.

"I don't care what it implies!" Helter snapped.

"Why can't we read the rest of the diary?" I shouted, grabbing for it. Pepper backed off. But it was Stan who put his hand on my arm.

"Calm down now, everyone," Stan said. "We won't read any more of the diary right now." He gestured to the loose pages on the desk. "We'll read her papers instead. Is that all right with everyone?"

"What if they're about us?" Leslie said softly as if she couldn't imagine anything more awful. Stan picked up the stack and thumbed through it.

"It just looks like a bunch of short stories to me," Stan said. "A page or two for each one."

"Stories," Leslie whispered.

We began to read.

LATI BALL PUTS ON A MASK

Lati Ball dressed for the costume party with relish. She wanted to look pretty. She wanted to look mysterious. She took a mask from the closet of witches and tied the lace bow around her sweet head. "My," she said as she stared into the mirror. "How happy we are to be the best. The men will ask me to dance. The men will forget the rest."

Lati Ball went to the dance. The mask fit tight on her soft face. The people did not recognize her, but said she was the best. "Oh, who is this woman?" they cried. "She walks like an angel and floats like a swan?" And the men lined up and asked for her hand. She was swept around the floor into another land.

The party went late and the night grew tired. Lati Ball had to stop and rest between dances. Then the clock rang twelve times and a cake was brought out. A cake of twelve candles. And Lati Ball wondered whose birthday it could be, and hurried to hear. The hostess of the party laughed and said, "The cake is for you! The cake is for the best! Take this knife now and cut some for the rest!"

But before Lati Ball could cut the cake, she wanted to make a wish. She leaned over the candles and said to herself, "I want always to be the best, better than the rest." Then she blew at the candles and blew at the cake. But the cake was made of wood and caught fire. It burned her mask. It burned her face. Then the mask was part of Lati Ball's face, and she looked like death.

Leslie let out a scream as we read the end of the story and grabbed the papers from Stan's hand. Before anyone could stop her, she had run from the room. We chased her into the kitchen. Pepper was the first to reach her. But she had already turned on the gas burners and thrown the story of Lati Ball into the flame. It had immediately caught. Fire licked at the sick words and smoke billowed around Leslie like a dark aura. She was crumpling up the next story when Pepper reached out to stop her. She grabbed the diary from Pepper and dropped the stories on the floor in the process. She showed the diary no mercy. She pressed it directly down on the blue flames on the stove. Pepper tried to pull her back and was rewarded with a hard kick to the shin. He bent over in pain. Leslie was determined. She was possessed. She pulled the book open on its side and let the fire slip into the cracks. The pages could have been soaked in gasoline. There was a flash of light and the room choked with another blast of black smoke.

"Stop!" Stan shouted. He leaped forward and knocked the diary off the stove and onto the floor. He began to stamp out the fire as Leslie also dropped down to the floor. She was after the pages again, and she had them in her hands in a second. Pepper grabbed at her once more. This time she poked him directly in the eye. He let go of her and screamed.

"You bitch!" I shouted at her, hurrying to Pepper's side. Leslie wasn't listening. She made a beeline for the back door, and was out in the yard before we could regroup. Stan was still trying to stomp out the burning diary. Helter was anxiously fingering the revolver in his belt and being about as helpful as a side of frozen beef.

"Are you all right?" I asked Pepper.

He grimaced. "I think so, dammit," he replied, his right hand over his left eyes. "Somebody stop her. She's going to hurt herself."

"Let her hurt herself," I said. I wanted to get a better look at Pepper's eye. I was worried. We didn't exactly have a lot of medical experience between the five of us.

"Get her," Stan said, close to extinguishing the diary, or what was left of it. "Get the stories."

It was up to me, I supposed. Giving Pepper a reassuring pat, I dashed out the back door. Leslie stood in the middle of the overgrown yard, tearing the pages into rough rectangles and sailing them on the wind, which had picked up considerably since we had entered the house. Leslie sang like a demented child. I didn't try to tackle her or anything. I didn't care that much for the stories anyway.

"Why are you doing this?" I asked in a bored voice. The scraps of paper blew over the fence and out of sight. They belonged to Salem now. Leslie stared at me gleefully.

"We're safe now," she babbled. "Betty Sue can't get us."

"Betty Sue's dead," I said. "She was never going to get anybody."

Leslie had finished with her shredding job. "That's what you think."

The guys appeared in another minute, Stan holding the tome of ash. Maybe a few pages of the diary had survived. Pepper had taken his hand down from his eye. It was horribly red, but not bleeding. Helter stood twitching beside them, trying to look important.

"Where are they?" Stan asked Leslie. She gestured to the sky.

"Gone," she said.

Stan was furious. "I told you to stop her," he said.

"Why?" I asked. "I didn't want to read any more of that crap." I glanced at Pepper. "I was more interested in her true life experiences."

"I only went out with her once," Pepper said again defensively.

"Why did you destroy the stories?" Stan asked Leslie.

She studied him as if he were slow. "You were her friend, too," she said. "You knew what she was."

"I didn't know her as well as you think," Stan said. "Why did the story of Lati Ball make you berserk?"

Leslie shook her head violently. "I can't talk about it. I'm not going to talk about her. I'm going to leave this town." She stared at Stan defiantly. "Don't try to stop me."

Stan shrugged. "Whatever you want."

Leslie turned to Pepper and tilted her head back, sizing him up. I hated her in that moment. I knew what she was going to say. The trouble was, I didn't know what my boyfriend would answer.

"Do you want to go with me?" Leslie asked Pepper.

Pepper glanced uncomfortably at me, and then at the ground. "Do you want to go, Rox?" he asked.

"No," I said, my voice cold. "But don't let me influence you."

Pepper's head snapped up. "I told you, I'm with you," he said.

"Tell *her* then," I said.

"Sorry," Pepper said to Leslie. His response surprised her. She shook off the rejection with a toss of her beautiful blond hair. She eyed Helter next.

"How about you?" Leslie asked. "Want to come?"

Helter was interested. The empty world was giving him a sexy blond all to himself to play with. "What would we do?" he asked.

"Go to L.A.," she said. "Have fun."

Helter nodded vigorously. "I'm in. This place sucks anyway."

"And what will you do in L.A.?" Stan asked.

"We'll live," Leslie said crossly. "Which is more than I think you'll do here."

Stan took a step toward her. "You have to tell us what you think is going on here. We have to work together."

Leslie was resolute. "No."

"Can't you at least tell us why these stories scared you so much?" Stan said.

Leslie smiled at the question. It was a curious smile because it was full of despair, without a hint of joy in it. She hung her head then and her hair fell forward, casting a shadow across her blue eyes. The ones that had sparkled in the dark.

"You'll find out," she said simply.

CHAPTER VII

STAN AND PEPPER AND I SAT ACROSS FROM THE GAS STATION where Leslie and Helter were making their final preparations to leave. They had found themselves a brand-new Ford Bronco. They had stocked it with guns and food and clothes. Now they were topping off the gas tank—and a spare tank they had wrestled into the back. They were afraid fuel might be short on the road, but I didn't believe it would be a problem.

"You know," I said to Stan and Pepper. "I freaked out this morning when I realized everyone was gone. But then I adjusted. I began to accept the idea. You two helped me. Maybe we did fall into another dimension. Maybe the saucers came and dumped us on the planet Zeon. I could handle all that. But now I've got another problem I can't handle. I feel like screaming."

"What is it?" Stan asked. The three of us were sitting on a curb—the three stooges, me in the middle. Stan continued to clutch the ravaged diary. Fifty yards away Helter and Leslie were doing their best to ignore us. They would be gone within minutes. Helter had the gas pump set on automatic and was busy checking the air pressure in the tires. Leslie was fiddling with something in the back of the Bronco, a cigarette in her mouth. I had never seen her smoke before. She had changed out of her pajamas and into black jeans and a tight red blouse.

"Well," I said. "We seem to have a strange girl—who happens to be dead—who grew up with exciting characters like Fat Freddy, and who put a hex on every boy who wouldn't kiss her. In fact, this same girl—who I might have seen hitchhiking this morning in the middle of nowhere—seems to have had a big effect on everyone who knew her intimately. A big *bad* effect." I paused and took a deep breath. "I was just wondering what the hell is happening and why isn't anyone telling me about it?" I smiled sweetly at Stan. "Do you see my problem?"

Stan nodded casually. "I don't know what the hell is going on either. Maybe we should both start screaming."

"But you, at least, have your suspicions," I said. "You're the one who dragged us straight to Betty Sue's house. Why? And forget what you told us in the ice-cream parlor. You wanted to go there from the word go."

Stan shrugged as if he were embarrassed. "I had this dream."

"What dream?" I asked. "When did you have it?"

"Four weeks ago, the night Betty Sue died," Stan said. He frowned. "It was in the middle of the night—it might have been just when she died."

"What was it about?" I asked.

"I was walking around town," Stan said. "It was

late and it was dark. The town was deserted, and I had a feeling it had been empty a long time. The wind was blowing in from the desert and sand was collecting on the streets, slowly burying them. I felt terribly lonely, but no matter how long and how far I walked I couldn't find anybody. Yet, at the same time, I had a constant feeling that I was being watched. I'd suddenly whirl around and catch a glimpse of a black shadow. But when I focused harder, there would be nothing there."

"How did the dream end?" I asked.

"It didn't end," Stan said. "It seemed to go on and on. That's what I remember most clearly—its timelessness. When I woke up it was still with me. Then I heard the news about Betty Sue." He shook his head. "Yeah, I guess that's what made me link our situation now with her. Good old Betty Sue."

"Let's get this straight," I said. "Do you think she was a witch or what?"

Stan seemed surprised. "Not that I know of. She was a writer."

"That we know already," Pepper said without enthusiasm.

"No," Stan said. "She was a wonderful writer. She showed me some of her stories. They were a lot better than that Lati Ball story."

"Did people always die in them?" I asked.

"Sometimes," Stan said. "Sometimes not. They were about all kinds of things: talking appliances, intelligent butterflies, time travelers from other galaxies." He paused and scratched his head. "But that Lati Ball tale was a strange one. It was short, and yet it kept repeating itself, almost as if she meant it more as a song."

"Or a chant," I said.

Stan nodded. "It had that kind of feel to it."

I rubbed my hands together impatiently. "You know, all the questions we've asked ourselves today, and all the answers we've come up with, have ultimately said nothing. So, let's get down to it. What was so special about Betty Sue? And what did she have to do with our predicament?"

"I honestly don't know," Stan said.

"How well did you know her?" I insisted.

He hesitated. "I was her friend. We were in chemistry together."

"Did you ever go out with her?" I asked.

"Not on a date." Stan gave a wry smile. "I'm the class nerd. Nerds don't go on dates. They're just happy if a girl wants them to help them with their homework."

"Did you help Betty Sue with her homework?" I asked.

"No," Stan said. "I let her copy off my test papers. It saved us both a lot of time. But don't get the wrong impression. She wasn't stupid. In fact I would say she was probably the only truly brilliant person in our class."

"You're that person," I protested.

Stan shook his head. "I'm clever, I'm not brilliant. True geniuses are rare. Betty Sue was a genius. You read only a sample of her writing. It was by no means her best stuff. But you must have felt the magic in it. When she wrote something, it was alive." Stan paused again, and now he was troubled. "It was almost as if her words had power."

"Leslie sure seems to think they do," I said, glancing over at our two would-be explorers. I wondered for a second what they'd find in L.A. I wondered if they'd even make it that far. Stan hadn't exactly said so, but I knew he believed there was no one left in the entire world except us.

"I wish she'd talk to us," Stan said, referring to Leslie.

"Maybe if we went with her she would," Pepper answered. He caught my eye and shook his head. "Whatever," he muttered.

"We still have to talk," I said.

"I have nothing to talk about," Pepper said flatly.

"I can leave," Stan volunteered.

"Don't," I said. "It's all right. It looks like we're all going to have plenty of time to talk, alone or together."

"That reminds me," Stan said. "I think you know what I'm going to ask."

"About this morning?" I asked.

"I don't mean to pry," Stan said carefully. "But these friends of yours in Foster . . ."

"We have no friends in Foster," I said. "Pepper and I were there on private business is all. But everything else was as I described."

"Did you talk to people there this morning?" Stan asked.

"Yes."

"You don't want to tell me who?" Stan asked. "I understand if you don't."

I smiled at Stan, although I didn't feel much like smiling. I trusted him. I should have just told him the truth and been done with it. But I didn't know how Pepper would react. "I'm glad you understand," I said.

Stan nodded. "That's fair."

"Would it be fair if I asked more about your last visit with Betty Sue?" I asked.

He thought a moment. "I'm going to have to ask for your understanding."

"It looks like Helter's ready to say goodbye to us," Pepper said, pointing. Armed and combat-ready for the enemy, Helter was lumbering across the road to pay his final respects. I continued to follow Leslie out of the corner of my eye. She had climbed out of the back of the Bronco and was trying to squeeze a few final drops into the main gas tank.

"You guys having any second thoughts?" Helter asked.

"Are you?" Pepper asked.

Helter pointedly glanced back at Leslie. "Hell, no. She's a babe. I would never have got a piece like her if there were people around."

"What if you meet other people?" I asked. "Other guys? Do you think Leslie's going to stay with you?"

Helter obviously hadn't thought of that. He fingered his jaw. "I guess I'll just have to impress her with my charm before we get to L.A."

"Are you taking Highway Ten?" Stan asked.

"I suppose," Helter said.

Stan checked the time. "It's three o'clock, and the sun seems to be crossing the sky at the same speed as usual. It'll be dark before you get there. Be careful on the road. There could be cars sitting right in the middle of the highway. It might be better if you didn't drive at night."

"You might want to stop and check into a motel," I said.

Helter grinned wolfishly. "Hey, as long as they don't ask me for a credit card we should be OK." He held out his hand to Pepper. "I'm sorry I shot your girlfriend. I'd like to part friends."

Pepper was surprised. He shook Helter's hand. "You listen to what Stan said," Pepper told him. "And when you get there, call my number. It's five-six-seven-nine. Just remember you start at five and you skip the eight. Leave a message if I'm not in."

"I'll call tonight and tell you what's out there," Helter said. He offered me his hand. "Rox."

"Helter," I said. And I don't know why, but I stood up and hugged him. "Don't go shooting any other pretty girls."

"Only if they shoot first," he said, giving me a strong squeeze. He let go and turned to Stan last. But Stan seemed preoccupied. He was watching Leslie intently. He didn't even hear when Helter said his name.

"Huh?" Stan mumbled finally.

"Saying goodbye," Helter said.

Stan blinked at him, then glanced back at Leslie. "Don't go just yet," he said.

Helter snorted. "We've talked about this till we're blue in the face. We want to go now while the sun's still up. Leslie won't spend another night in this town." He offered Stan his hand. "We'll talk on the phone, if they keep working."

Stan held on to Helter's hand and didn't let go. He was suddenly uneasy. "Helter," Stan said. "Listen to me. Something's wrong—I can't quite place it. You have to give me a minute."

Helter laughed and shook him off. "You're a great guy, but you think too much, Stan. Me and Leslie are going to have some fun. We're going out on the town." He turned away. "Stay healthy."

We watched him go. Stan especially. He kept his eyes locked on Helter, and Leslie, and the gas station. And I followed his lead. The Bronco tank had to be overflowing by now, I thought. Leslie pulled the nozzle out of the tank and started to place it back on the pump. But she still had that goddamn cigarette in her mouth, and as far as we all knew, she didn't smoke that much. It was a dirty habit anyway. It ruined your lungs. It gave you cancer. It cut short your life. It made you cough. Particularly when you were just starting to smoke again.

Leslie coughed as she hung up the dripping pump.

The cigarette popped out of her mouth.

It fell on the ground and rolled out of sight.

Stan leapt to his feet.

"Leslie," he cried and started running toward the station, toward tough dude Helter and Salem High's all-American beauty. Stan was fifteen feet from Helter and seventy feet from the gas station when the orange flame suddenly snaked up Leslie's side of the Bronco. It looked like no big deal at first. Just a little fire and smoke. But the snake was in a hurry. It had places to go. Leslie watched it crawl right up to the opening of the gas tank. I knew she shouldn't have overfilled the thing and splashed so much around. The fumes are what ignite. Leslie stared dumbfounded, then jerked her head over in our direction.

Right then Leslie's world exploded.

The tank in the Bronco went first. An orange ball of death shelling out glowing mangled steel. It was enough as far as Leslie was concerned. The shock wave slammed her into the pump and the flames and metal ripped through her torso. Just like that her story was over. Eighteen years of school and acting and the best shampoo. Just wasted. Smoke. God.

Stan was smart. He saw what was coming. He slammed into Helter and they both fell to the ground just as the *huge* tank beneath the burning pump met the flames. This fire ball was atomic. The shock wave hit Pepper and me like the hammer of Thor. We were knocked off the curb and on to our backs. For a moment thought was blown from my mind, and I could hear nothing. I don't know how long I lay there. I know my eyes were closed as Pepper pulled me to my feet. My eyes popped open.

"Are you all right?" he shouted. I knew he was shouting, even though he sounded far away. My ears weren't really ringing—it was more like I was under-water.

"Yes!"

"What?"

I nodded. "Yes!"

He nodded. "Good!"

We turned toward Helter and Stan. They were

getting up slowly. The shock wave must have hit them really hard. If Helter had been standing, he would have died. We all stared at one another for a minute, our faces as blank as those of fish dragged into the open air with hooks in their mouths. Why look over anyway? So we could see what was left of Leslie, if anything? But people are sick. I know I am. I looked, we all did.

We saw hell. We saw an eviscerated Ford Bronco. Gas pumps that fumed like stumps of sulphur. Billowing flames that rent the air like angry whips. The shattered concrete was a volcanic fissure. But did we see Leslie? Maybe a part of her. It lay beside a melting tire, smoking. This is too sick. It might have been a leg.

"I would never have got a piece like her if there were people around."

Helter had just been being Helter.

But still—I couldn't bear it.

I turned away and gagged on vomit that never passed my lips.

I heard Stan speak behind me, from far away.

"Lati Ball blew out her candles," he said.

CHAPTER VIII

WE SAT IN THE CENTER OF THE TOWN SQUARE. HALF AN hour had passed since the cremation of Leslie Belle. Off to the south, in the direction of the gas station, the smoke continued to rise. The station was somewhat isolated and Stan believed the fire wouldn't spread.

Stan sat with the charred diary of Betty Sue resting on his lap. He turned what was left of the pages carefully. Pepper and Helter sat and did nothing. None of us had spoken in a while. I figured I might as well be the first.

"I hope she didn't feel anything," I said.

"She didn't know what hit her," Stan said.

I remembered her stricken expression as she looked over at us. "She knew," I said.

More silence. More wind. It blew out of the south. The direction had not changed since the day had begun. South—the general direction of Foster and the abortion clinic. The wind brought the sand, and the sand scratched at my skin like invisible pelting rain. I could smell the smoke from where we sat. The gas station also lay to the south.

I didn't know how to grieve for Leslie. I hadn't known her that well. I had liked her—in our other world. But in this world, this place with no people, her death seemed somehow surreal. Or perhaps it was the reverse. It had seemed quite natural that she should have gone. I know that sounds terrible, but it was true. The silence was so alive—it was as if it couldn't tolerate any living things disturbing it.

I wondered if the silence would come for more of us.

"This thing is really hard to read," Stan said, his face close to the diary.

"Can you read any of it?" I asked.

He nodded. "Bits." He glanced at Helter and Pepper. "Not much."

"Does she always sound crazy?" I asked.

"Yes and no," Stan said. "She was definitely unusual." Stan set the diary aside. "I'm more interested now in reading the stories that were on those loose pages."

"Why?" I asked.

Stan shrugged. "If I tell you what I think, you'll think I'm crazy."

"Try us," Pepper said.

Stan looked at the distant smoke. "Leslie died like Lati."

"No, she didn't," I said. "It was totally different."

Stan shook his head. "It was the same. The story was a metaphor for Leslie."

"I don't see the connection at all," I said, lying. What he was saying spooked me like nothing that had happened since that morning. And I think it was because he had finally touched upon a "truth."

"Did you know Leslie when she was young?" Stan asked us all.

"I didn't live here," Pepper said.

"I'd see her around town," I said.

"I knew her," Helter said. Of all of us, he was the most upset over what had happened to her, and I don't think it was just because he had lost his source of sexual delight. He had wept as the flames streamed before us. He just kept saying over and over again, "She was so beautiful. She was so beautiful." But not in a crude way. I believe the possibility of going off with her had meant more to him than any of us could imagine.

"I knew her," Stan said. "She wasn't nearly as cute as she was later on."

"So?" I asked. "That's common. People blossom."

"She blossomed a lot," Stan said.

"Yeah," Helter said, showing interest. "She was ugly when she was a kid. I used to throw rocks at her."

"Wait a second," Pepper interrupted. "I want to stop this before it goes any further. Betty Sue had nothing to do with Leslie being pretty."

"I don't think he's saying that," I told my boyfriend.

"Maybe I am," Stan said. "Remember what she said in her diary. 'I have done so much for her. I made her what she is.'"

Pepper got up and paced in front of us. "I cannot accept any of this. Everyone has disappeared—all right, that's weird. Logic can't explain it. But to make a suicidal young woman into some kind of sorcerer is ridiculous."

"Sorcerer," Stan said. "That's an interesting choice of words."

"She was no sorcerer!" Pepper said.

"I'm not saying she was," Stan said. "Except to say she was very unusual. But let's talk a bit about Leslie, and Lati. Helter can tell you, Leslie was unattractive up until she was about fourteen. Now I know she was going through puberty, and I understand about the whole hormone thing. But the change in her was extraordinary. Leslie hit fourteen and suddenly glowed."

"I often thought that about her," I said.

Stan nodded. "Leslie was the closest of us to Betty Sue. They grew up together. They shared secrets—the diary says that much. In fact, it sounds like they shared peculiar secrets. Of all of us, Leslie was the most terrified of Betty Sue. She was terrified of what Betty Sue had written. It was as if she knew Betty Sue had power."

"What power?" I asked.

"Isn't it obvious?" Stan asked. "To make things happen."

"Stop!" Pepper pleaded.

"Did you ever see any demonstration of her power?" I asked.

"Not exactly," Stan said.

"What does that mean?" I asked. "Did you or didn't you?"

Stan fingered the burnt diary, his touch almost loving. It struck me then that Stan had cared for Betty Sue a great deal, perhaps even loved her. "I would go to see her for no reason on the spur of the moment," he said. "And she would always be there, waiting for me. She'd smile and say she brought me there."

"Anybody can say anything," Pepper said.

Stan shook his head sadly. "I wouldn't really want to go but I would anyway."

"Why wouldn't you want to go?" I asked.

"Maybe because I was afraid of her, too," Stan said.

"What was she like?" I asked. "From what I remember she was always alone."

"She was shy and soft spoken," Stan said. "That might be hard to believe from what you read of her diary, but people can write at length about things they wouldn't even think around other people. She was polite. But there was something about her . . . " He stopped.

"What?" I asked.

Stan slowly made a fist, his gaze focused in the far distance. "I don't like talking about things like this now."

"You think it might be dangerous?" I asked.

He looked at me. "Yes."

"Tell us your big story," Pepper said impatiently.

Stan glanced up in surprise. "It's not a big story. It's really a small thing what I was going to say. But I guess it's revealing." He took a breath. "Once when I went to see her, she was in the backyard, collecting butterflies in big glass jars. There were a lot of flowers in her yard and butterflies gathered there. She would hum a song—it seemed to bring them nearer to her. Then she'd trap them in her jars, and screw on the lids, and leave them alone."

"That doesn't sound particularly cruel," I said,

imagining that he was going to tell us that she stuck needles through their bodies, or something ghoulish like that. He swallowed uneasily before he continued, however, and I realized in that pause that Betty Sue would never have been so obvious.

"The lids had nail holes punched in them," Stan said. "There was plenty of air for the butterflies. She had dozens of jars. She would collect dozens of butterflies. But then she would leave the jars out in the backyard and just sit and watch the butterflies die."

"Why would they die?" I asked.

"Because she would leave them in the sun," Stan said. "You're all familiar with the greenhouse effect. The air inside the jars would slowly heat up and kill the butterflies. But that wasn't what would get me. It was the way she'd talk as she watched them die. 'You see, Stan,' she'd say, 'butterflies are dumb. They don't even know when they're in a glass jar. They can see everything just the same. And because of that, they think they can fly wherever they want, like always. But inside my jars they're only allowed to fly in tiny circles.' Then she leaned over and smiled at me and said, 'People are a lot like butterflies, don't you think, Stan?'"

"What did you say to her?" I asked, feeling sick to my stomach.

"I said what I thought," Stan said. "That butterflies and people had little in common that I could see. That made her laugh. She said, 'To you maybe. But not to me.'"

"Is there a moral to this story?" Pepper asked.

Stan spoke firmly. "Leslie was a plain girl with zero

charisma. Almost overnight she became a beautiful young lady. I believe Betty Sue gave her that beauty. I don't know how. I don't know why. And I also believe Betty Sue took away that beauty. I believe Betty Sue killed Leslie."

"Betty Sue is dead!" Pepper shouted.

"She may be dead," Stan said. "Or she may be alive. We can't be sure. Her body was never positively identified. But in either case, her work lives on."

"Her stories?" I asked, trying to put this all together.

"Yes," Stan said.

"And you believe all this just because you'd go over to her house even when you didn't want to?" Pepper asked sarcastically.

"That's just one of the reasons," Stan said. "But look at her story of Lati Ball. Notice the initials are the same as Leslie Belle's? That story was about Leslie, and Leslie knew it. That was why she was so anxious to destroy it. She knew the power of Betty Sue's pen. Betty Sue gave Leslie a mask so that she could be the best. That was Leslie's beauty. Then Betty Sue destroyed the mask with her 'candles.' Did any of you ever see Leslie smoke before? Of course you didn't. Leslie didn't smoke. She only started today because she had to."

"What do you mean, she *had* to?" I asked. "Was she *commanded?*"

"I believe so," Stan said.

"I hope she didn't write a story about me," Helter said. From the quaver in his voice he was obviously buying everything Stan was laying down. I wasn't. I mean, I felt Stan had insight into the situation, and I didn't think he was making stuff up just to scare us. But he had turned Betty Sue into a Jedi Knight who had gone over to the dark side. If I bought that scenario, I thought, then I might as well go wait in the car for her to come and drive me off the side of the planet.

Yet looking around at an empty planet made it impossible for me to dismiss Stan out of hand. The more he spoke, the more I felt like I was falling into a silent void where gravity wasn't the only thing pulling me down. Maybe the car would come to pick me up, after all, and Betty Sue would be behind the wheel. Smiling.

"Lati Ball," I whispered. "I wonder what she called each of us?"

"We'll never know," Pepper said in dismissal. "And it doesn't matter."

Stan stood. "We can know. We can try to find the pieces of paper that Leslie tore up and fit them back together."

Pepper grabbed Stan. "You're going too far."

Stan just looked at him. "She was strange, Pepper. She was almost more strange than a dead planet."

"But you liked her?" Pepper said.

Stan nodded. "She was childlike inside, too. I liked that part of her."

Pepper regarded him closely. "What did she *do* for you?" he asked.

Stan sighed. "Nothing, I hope."

CHAPTER IX

WE STARTED AT BETTY SUE'S HOUSE, IN THE BACKYARD, where Leslie had stood dancing in the sun earlier and singing about how the wicked witch couldn't get us anymore. The wind had died down somewhat—perhaps out of respect for our search. There were a few scraps of paper caught on the back fence and Stan gathered those up first and studied them closely. But they were too little and too few to tell a tale. We had to move on to the next backyard, and into the next street, searching for bits of the notebook pages. Yeah, we all thought Stan had gone way out on a limb with his Betty Sue obsession, but we were going to search for those pieces of paper as long as the sun was up.

And maybe even into the night.

'Cause there was nothing else to do.

The madness began around five-thirty. We had talked so much about Betty Sue that maybe only our minds' eye saw it. I am only sorry that it had to be me who screamed first.

I did see her, though. I saw Betty Sue.

I think.

We were moving around a house, Pepper and I. Stan and Helter were across the street, picking through the bushes. It was only after I saw what I did that I realized we were circling Leslie's house. Maybe it was a coincidence.

Anyway, Pepper had just spotted a scrap of our paper stuck on a branch in a tree and was reaching up to free it when I turned toward the bathroom window of the house. It was one of those fat fuzzy windows that make you look disfigured no matter how beautiful you are. I stared at it a second, blinking, because I thought I saw something move behind it. There was nothing there. A moment later it appeared again, a head of bright red hair swept across the glass. No one in Salem, except Betty Sue, had had hair that color. The image was just there for a second.

I should have screamed then. But I wasn't sure what I'd just seen. I didn't want to make a fool of myself. I glanced over at Pepper. He was preoccupied. I decided to take a closer look. I should have known better. I'd seen enough horror movies to know that the absolute worst thing you can do is to go off and investigate on your own. But that's what I did. I stepped around the back of the house and turned the knob on the door. It was open. I stepped inside. The late Leslie Belle's house.

"Hello?" I called.

Deep silence. Betty Sue's calling card. A silence so sharp it could cut. I moved forward, through the kitchen and into a hallway that I instinctively knew led to the bathroom. I felt something tighten around my throat. A garrote of silver wire spun from a nightmare recorded in black ink on a page of white notebook paper. But the feeling was only in my mind. Betty Sue's stories were only in her mind. Why should her mind have the right to overlap with mine? I hardly knew her, I thought. What was *our* common denominator?

Then I stood in the bathroom before a drawn shower curtain. The thick fuzzy window stood behind the curtain, and beyond that was the outside, where there were trees and sunshine. I lined up the order of things in my mind so that I would know if there was something in between them that wasn't supposed to be there. Like a dead girl.

I pulled back the curtain.

There was nothing.

Nothing but a whisper—at my back.

I whirled. But there was nothing.

Except a shadow in the bathroom mirror.

A moving shadow of red and black. Moving out of sight.

Was it Betty Sue? I don't know. I didn't care.

I screamed.

That brought the guys. Pepper found me first, but before I could get my voice back, Helter and Stan were in the hallway as well. I must have screamed pretty loud.

"What is it?" Pepper demanded.

I pointed a shaky arm. "She was here."

"Who?" Stan said.

"Her," I gasped.

105

"Who's her?" Pepper asked.

"The witch," I said. I stared at each of them. "I saw her."

"Are you sure?" Stan asked me.

I nodded. "I saw something, I swear it." I grabbed Pepper's arm with one hand. My other hand was stuffed full of scraps of Betty Sue's notebook pages. "God, she's alive."

Helter cocked his rifle. "Let's get her."

"No, wait," Stan said. "We're not going to shoot her."

"We're not," Helter said. "I am. Pepper, are you coming?"

"Where am I coming?" Pepper asked. "Where is she?"

"Don't go," I told him. Pepper let go of my arm.

"I've got to," he said. "Now where did you see her?"

I gestured helplessly. "Just here. Through the window. In the mirror. I don't know."

"She's dead meat," Helter swore, scanning the area with beady eyes.

I turned to Stan. "Stop them," I pleaded.

"We'll look for her together," Stan said. "No violence."

We left the hallway for the front of the house. Leslie's place was a simple two story, about twice the size of Betty Sue's. Helter's trigger finger was sweating. He ran ahead of us and up the stairs out of sight, Pepper not far behind. Stan had lost control of the group.

"Who the hell let that guy carry a gun?" Stan cursed, his extra weight slowing him down.

As if in response, a shot was fired.

"Oh, no," I moaned.

We caught up with Helter and Pepper in an upstairs bedroom. Double doors leading onto a small balcony were lying wide open. There was a bullet hole through the center of the right door. "I almost got her," Helter cried, peering out the side of the door. Pepper crouched by his side.

"Did you see her?" Pepper asked.

"Sure," Helter said. "Didn't you see her?"

"I don't know," Pepper said. "I saw a red and black blur."

"That was her," Helter said.

Stan strode straight to the balcony door and looked straight out. "I don't see anything," he said.

"She was here," Helter exclaimed. He jumped out onto the balcony and surveyed the length of the street. "She must have ducked into another yard."

"Are you sure you saw her?" Stan asked.

"Do you think I'm seeing things?" Helter asked, insulted. He was breathing hard. Sweat stained his shirt, and he had a wild-eyed, vacant look, as if no one was home. That vacantness had begun with the explosion at the gas station.

"I think it's possible," Stan said. "How did she get off the roof?"

"She climbed down," Helter said. He shook his head in confusion and disgust. "You're the one who's been telling us all along that she's a witch. Well, I believe you now! We've got to get her before she gets us." He shielded his eyes from the twilight sun low in the sky and peered across the street. Then suddenly he jumped up and pointed. "There she is! Right there! Come on, Pepper."

Helter and my boyfriend dashed downstairs, anxious to slay the evil monster. I didn't see anybody across the street, but I had started to chase after them when Stan put a hand on my arm to stop me.

"Let them go," he said. "There's nobody there."

"But I already saw her," I protested.

"I believe you," Stan said.

"Then what are you saying?" I asked.

He gestured to the scraps of paper I had collected. I had Pepper's pile as well now. I handed them over. Stan stared at them a moment and then indicated we should follow the guys after all. We went downstairs and outside. Stan still had the burnt diary, tucked into his belt. "Maybe I can piece together a story or two in the meantime," he said.

The guys had disappeared into a neighbor's backyard. Stan and I were halfway across the street when another shot rang out. My heart jumped into my mouth. Stan remained calm. In the distance Helter howled in disgust.

"She could be here," I said. "If half of what you say is true."

"Oh, she's here," Stan said, studying the scraps as if they were pieces of a puzzle, which indeed they were. "But she's not going to be caught by Helter and his gun. This is her story."

"You're talking about how she was able to make things happen by writing about them?"

"Yes."

"Did she write us into this empty world?"

Stan stopped for a moment as he fitted a piece against another one. "That's what I believe."

"Why?" I asked anxiously. I couldn't say I agreed with him, but I no longer disagreed with him, which is about halfway toward belief—I guess. *Something* had moved inside the bathroom window, and it had had red hair.

"Do you mean, why us?" Stan asked. "Or why do this to anybody?"

"Both questions."

"Except for you, we all knew her," Stan said, still fiddling with the pages. "We all must have done something to hurt her. Let's take Leslie for example. It's not hard to figure out how she pissed Betty Sue off. When they were young they were best friends. But we saw in the diary how when Leslie grew up, she stole the boys Betty Sue was interested in away from her."

"What about the rest of you?" I asked.

"Just a second, I might be able to give you something specific." Stan stopped again. This time he sat on the curb and arranged his scraps on the asphalt and held them together with tape he had taken from Betty Sue's room. Down the street I could see Helter and Pepper running and shouting to each other, jumping fences and pointing. Perhaps it was because of what Stan had just said, but I suddenly had the strong impression that they were behaving like puppets.

"I think we now have a story about Helter," Stan said, taping the last of the scraps together.

I came around and peered over his shoulder. I had to squint; Stan had sat in the shade and the sun was falling toward the western horizon. Less than two hours and it would be dark. For the moment the wind had died down to the gentlest of breezes. The scraps belonged together—the page was complete.

"Before we read it all the way through," Stan said. "I want to tell you something about Helter and Betty Sue's relationship. I gleaned this from what was left of the diary. Because of all the damage, I can't give you exact details. But I'm quite sure I'm correct."

"Correct about what?" I asked.

"Helter raped Betty Sue."

"God. Are you sure she didn't *make* him do it?"

Stan nodded. "You're beginning to think like me. And there could be some truth in what you're suggesting. I think Betty Sue taunted him toward committing the act. But then, I think he caught even her by surprise. Her tone, in the bits and snatches I could put together, was very angry."

"Then she can't be all powerful," I said. "If she couldn't control Helter."

Stan glanced toward the lowering sun. When he spoke there was nothing but despair in the sound of his voice. "She couldn't control the butterflies," he said softly. "Until she put them in her jar."

I sat beside him and shivered. It was ironic that here we were in the midst of a mystical discussion and down the street Pepper and Helter were locked in what they thought was a life-and-death pursuit. I just hoped Helter didn't accidentally shoot Pepper. I lowered my head.

"Let's read her story," I said.

We read in silence.

HOLT SKATER TAKES A WALK

Holt Skater lived beside a stone wall that was both wide and tall. He would look up at it each day as he walked to his farm field. And he would say to himself, "It is not so tall that I could not climb it. Not this wall." Holt did not like the field where he had to work and toil in the mud and soil. He did not like it at all and wanted to escape over the tall wall.

One day he noticed a tree beside the wall, a tree that was very tall. And he climbed the tree and jumped onto the wall, and glimpsed the other side. There he saw streams and fields, where the food would be easy to pick for frequent meals. But at the foot of the wall he saw thorn bushes instead of fields, and he could not climb down and walk beside the streams. Then he said to himself, "I will walk along the wide wall until I come to a tree that is tall." He thought then he could climb down onto the other side, and forget his work and hide.

Holt went for a long walk along the wall. He walked and walked and forgot the other side of the wall, and the tree that helped him up, the tree that was tall. But the thorn bushes did not stop and he began to grow hot. He had walked so far without a hat, and he wished he could go back. But he looked and the thorn bushes were now on both sides, and he knew if he jumped into them they would tear his hide. He turned around, and tried to go back along the wall without a hat. But the wall stayed tall without staying wide. And soon the wall was so narrow it was like a walk on a dangerous ride. The wall got narrower and narrower and he said to himself, "I do not understand how I could have turned around and not gotten back."

Holt was now scared and he began to shake. He knew if the wall got too narrow he would fall off and the thorns would get him like a rake. He turned back again, the other way, and the wall narrowed more so that he was now sure he would fall and be sore. Then he turned once more and the wall became like a razor and he began to cry for someone to be his savior. But it was too late for Holt, who had brains that were like steel bolts. The wall was now a razor that could cut like laser. And Holt finally slipped, one leg this way, and one leg that way. And what happened to him is not easy to say. He fell and fell and prayed to Jesus. But in the end he was just a bloody mess made up of two pieces.

"Sick!" I cried when we finished.

"Helter Skelter," Stan said. "Holt Skater."

"What's going to happen to him?" I asked, and there were tears in my eyes. I didn't believe any of it.

Witchcraft, sorcery, curses—it was all B.S. But Betty Sue's stories—the way they were worded, the rhymes, the endings—they had gotten inside me. And I couldn't get them out, any more than a butterfly could get out of a sealed jar.

"Helter raped Betty Sue," Stan said. "I'm sure she's thought up something special for him."

"When you thumbed through the pile of papers on Betty Sue's desk, the story of Lati Ball was on top. What story was second?"

"I believe it was the one we just read," Stan said.

I jumped to my feet. "Let's get Helter. Let's not let him out of our sight."

Stan got up slower. "Do you believe me? What I said about her?"

I hesitated. "Yes."

He seemed relieved for a second, but then his face fell. "What difference does it make?"

"It does make a difference. We have to know what's going on. Only that way can we prevent it." I paused. "We *can* stop it, can't we?"

He smiled at me. He had a nice smile. He was a nice guy. I had just reassured him and now I was asking for his reassurance. "I'm sure there must be a way," he said. He held up the remainder of the scraps of papers we had collected so far. "We need to get the rest of these stories together."

"Let's get Helter first," I said. We started up the street in the direction of the boys. But I stopped after a minute. "Stan? Was there any more mention of Pepper in Betty Sue's diary?" I asked.

It was Stan's turn to hesitate. "Yes."

"What did she say about him?"

"I could only pick out bits and pieces," he said.

"Come on. What did he do to her?"

Stan was stubborn. "I don't know. Ask Pepper. He'd know."

"Yeah," I said thoughtfully. "I suppose he would."

CHAPTER X

WE CAUGHT UP WITH HELTER AND PEPPER AS THEY WERE nearing Salem High. They were excited. They had caught sight of Betty Sue three times. Sort of. She moved fast, they said. The way they talked, she must have been riding a broom. Stan tried to reason with them.

"Why haven't you been able to catch her?" Stan asked.

"She's too slippery," Helter said, his eyes practically bulging out of his head. He still had his rifle and revolver. Obviously he wasn't about to share his weapons with Pepper.

"She went into the school," Pepper said with conviction. He pointed toward the administration building at the front of the campus. Between the building and us was the teachers' parking lot, an asphalt square a hundred feet away.

"Honey, she's not really there," I said.

Pepper had gone from being a skeptic to a believer quick. But I could understand that. There had been something between him and Betty Sue. His guilt had

115

confirmed that long before Leslie died. He had tried to deny it as best he could—while there was a chance. But now that Betty Sue had appeared he wanted her silenced immediately. He pointed at the teachers' parking lot.

"Do you see those footprints?" he asked.

The wind had swept a quarter inch of sand onto the lot. It would have been impossible to cross it without leaving tracks. Perhaps Betty Sue couldn't do the impossible or maybe it was just part of her plan. In either case footprints stretched all the way across the asphalt to the front steps of the school.

"Those don't belong to you guys?" Stan asked, and even he seemed amazed.

"They're hers, dammit," Helter said. He cocked his rifle. He was forever cocking it. I think it was a macho thing to do. "Let's get her."

"You are not going to shoot her," Stan told him.

"I'll take her alive," Helter said grimly. "If she lets me."

We started forward. I couldn't believe what was happening. Perhaps that would keep me from seeing her—my lack of belief. But I could see her footprints clearly enough. I traced them as I walked, and from the distance between them it didn't appear that Betty Sue had been in a hurry as she crossed the parking lot.

Pepper was wrong about Betty Sue having gone into the administration building. A fine coat of sand covered the entire campus. It was clear her steps led around to the back of the campus. It was so easy to follow her, it made me suspicious. I wondered if she was leading us into a trap.

My suspicions leapfrogged near the gymnasium when the tracks suddenly split and went in two separate directions. We stared at them dumbfounded. One veered toward the back of the gym, the other toward the girls' showers.

"How did she do that?" Helter asked.

Stan squatted and studied both sets of prints in the sand. "These were made by someone wearing boots," he muttered.

"So?" Pepper asked. "Who cares?"

Stan looked up. "She had boots on when she died."

I chuckled. "So? We know now her body in the fire was a hoax."

Stan stood. "It was a real body."

"Look," Helter said, agitated. "Let's talk later. She's getting away. Let's split up. Pepper, you and Rox follow the prints leading to the gym. Stan and I will search the girls' showers."

"We shouldn't split up," Stan said sternly.

"We have to split up!" Helter shouted. "Let's just do it."

I put my hand on Helter's shoulder. "We can split up if I can go with you," I told him.

"Rox?" Pepper said.

"It's nothing personal," I said, catching Stan's eye.

"I don't care who comes with me," Helter said, raising his rifle and striding forward. "As long as they don't get in my way."

"This is a mistake," Stan said, resigned to the decision.

I followed Helter, but had to jog to keep up with him. We chased the impressions in the sand to the green metal door leading to the showers. They stopped there, of course. The door was unlocked but closed over. Helter pulled it back. There was no sand inside. No wind. It was dark and cool, and my skin cringed as the door slowly closed behind us. I had never liked gym. I hated exercise. I hated to shower in front of other girls. I hated gym teachers. I got very poor grades in the class.

"Do you hear anything?" I whispered to Helter.

"Shh," he said. He touched my hand and scanned the rows of lockers. "She's here."

"How do you know?" I asked.

He drew in a shuddering breath. "I feel her." He looked at me. "I feel what I felt at the gas station before Leslie died."

"What was that?"

"Evil," he said.

We continued forward. The dark was damp, and the faint smell of sweat that hung in the air was like a memory of carefree times. An open bathroom door yawned black on our left, the closed gray lockers stretched out on our right. I indicated the bathroom and Helter shook his head. I was relieved. I didn't want to go in there either.

We were beside the gym teacher's office when Helter made me halt. "What is it?" I asked.

He leaned his head to the side. "Did you hear that?"

"What?"

"It was the sound of wood bumping against wood." He paused. "I think she's in the equipment cage."

"I didn't hear anything."

He put a finger to my lips. "You stay here. I want to investigate."

I brushed his finger aside. "We have to stick together."

He leaned in close and spoke in my ear. "I know she's in there, Roxanne. I know why she's there. I hurt her once, now she wants to hurt me. I can't take you with me."

"She made you hurt her," I said, grabbing his arm. "Listen to me, we shouldn't even be in here alone. Let's go get the others. We can be out and back in two minutes."

He let his hand slide down to the trigger on his rifle. He was petrified—that was obvious—but he also appeared to be resolved to face whatever lay around the corner. "No," he said.

"She'll kill you," I hissed. "Your story was next."

His eyes met mine. The news didn't seem to surprise him. "We'll see who gets killed." He gently pushed me down onto one of the long wooden benches that ran in front of the lockers. "Stay here."

I let him walk away. I don't know why. I shouldn't have. Yeah, actually I do know why. I was scared. Helter vanished in the dark.

I sat there feeling like a coward, so I got back up. Yet I didn't feel like chasing after Helter, or entering the equipment locker. I was afraid he might accidentally shoot me. I decided to swing around the back of the locker room, through the showers to see what was there.

I sneaked up the narrow aisle on my toes. The pale

twilight coming in through the high dirty windows was of small help. Once I stumbled and banged my shin. The shock made me recoil in pain. I had almost forgotten about the bullet wound in my right thigh.

The showers waited for me in shadow. I stepped hastily inside and hugged the tile wall as I scampered toward the far end. I could hear my heart pounding, my breath coming in ragged gasps, and nothing else. It seemed to take forever to reach the far end. I think the main reason was because as I walked, I was burdened with memory.

A memory of Betty Sue.

There was no mystery why it came to me right then and there. My only real encounter with Betty Sue had occurred in these showers. We didn't have gym class together, and I still don't know why she was playing volleyball with us that day. But she must have had a reason—maybe she was making up a class. Anyway, she was good at the game. A slender and tall girl, she had quick reflexes and excellent coordination. She was on my team, and she was the main reason we won. But her skills didn't make her popular. The whole period, I doubted if the other girls said five words to her. I know I hardly even looked at her. I hated being out there on the volleyball court when I could be lying on my bed at home listening to the radio.

But the few times I did glance over at her I remember wondering how she got her curly hair so bright. The color certainly didn't look natural.

Then class was over and we went inside to shower. Betty Sue and I were the last two girls to get under the water—the gym teacher had made us collect all the balls and put them away in the equipment locker. She took a shower not far or close to mine. Once more, I hardly looked over at her. I didn't want her to think I was queer or anything. But I did see enough of her to know she wasn't simply thin, but bony—almost to the point of starvation. She was also extremely pale.

She finished with her shower first, but didn't walk out the way she had come in. She deliberately walked past me, and handed me a bar of soap. I grunted "thank you" and paid the gesture little heed, until Betty Sue was out of sight; then I glanced down at the soap. I could hardly believe what I saw. A baby, a crying baby, in exquisite detail had been carved into the face of the bar. It could have been an artist's square of ivory she handed me.

I had known Pepper about a week then, and I was pregnant, although I didn't know it. Betty Sue would be dead in less than a week.

I walked out the same way Betty Sue had vanished. I wanted to ask her where she had gotten the soap. It appeared to be a one-of-a-kind item; the figure of the baby had clearly not been preformed with the bar, but had been carved in later. I peered around the edge of the showers and saw Betty Sue drying herself in front of a mirror. At least that's what I thought she was doing at first. I stopped myself from speaking when I saw she was drawing on the naked reflection of herself in the mirror with another bar of soap. This bar was dyed red. In fact, the soap was the same shade of red as Betty Sue's hair when her hair was wet. Mixed with water, the soap dripped off the mirror like running blood.

I didn't say anything. I just dropped my bar on the floor and walked away, sick to my stomach. Betty Sue had been soaping her reflection in the area of her stomach.

And that's what I remembered as I paused in the dark. To my left was the mirror where Betty Sue had colored her reflection. It was dark, and my own reflected image was even darker. Betty Sue had stood out as a silhouette against the sun this morning, and now that the sun was going down I stood as a shadow of that day almost five weeks earlier. I could distinguish the faint outline of the dyed soap on the mirror still. Betty Sue had drawn a jar around her reflected belly. What did she pretend to fill this one with, I wondered?

Helter screamed. A shot rang out.

"Oh, no," I cried.

I spun and ran in the direction of the noise. Another shot tore the dark, followed in quick succession by two others. And all the while Helter screamed as if an alien monster with claws and tentacles and teeth as long as knives was bearing down on him. Coming at him without a pause. Impervious to his shots.

He screamed like someone dying.

But when I finally saw him, he was all in one piece. He'd had his rifle out and was blasting away. In the flash of the bullets I saw and heard glass shatter at the far end of the building. In an instant I realized what was happening. He had glimpsed his own reflection in the big primping mirror by the exit and spooked himself.

"Helter!" I called.

He shrieked. He didn't hear me. He fired once more, and his bullet ricocheted dangerously. Then I heard the clicking of his empty trigger as he tried to unload shells that were no longer in the chamber. He stumbled backward, as if before a towering beast. Then he fell and landed on his butt and squirmed back against a bench that wasn't going to move out of the way for him. Desperately he reached for the revolver in his belt.

"Helter!" I screamed. "She's not there!"

Too late. He grabbed the revolver. Too soon he fired it. He must have been out of his mind with fear. He grabbed the revolver and the trigger and accidentally shot himself while the gun was still in his belt.

"Ahh!" he cried.

The revolver fell from his hand onto the concrete floor as he rolled into a ball of agony. I was at his side in a moment. I tried to hold him, to comfort him, but he kept thrashing. The door flew open behind me and remained open. It was Stan and Pepper. A shaft of evening light shone down on Helter through the open door. The top of his pants was soaked dark red. I couldn't help but remember Stan's prediction.

"Helter raped Betty Sue. I'm sure she's thought up something special for him."

Helter had shot himself in the groin.

"Oh, Jesus," I moaned, my hands already soaked with his blood. "Help him."

Stan and Pepper ran to Helter's side. Stan tried to roll him over on his back so that he could figure out the extent of the injury, but Helter was in too much pain. He kept shaking violently.

"It's no good," he cried. "It's no good."

"You're going to be all right," Stan said, and there wasn't a whisper of truth in the words and he knew it. Helter clawed Stan's hand, the veins on his neck bulging like wires, his contorted features drenched with sweat. He was crying and I was crying and it was horrible.

"Kill me," Helter begged Stan.

Stan shook his head, shocked. "We're going to help you. We're not going to kill you."

Helter started to sob. "Do you know where I've been shot? You have to kill me. I'll die anyway." He reached feebly for his revolver but Stan pulled it away. "Please," Helter pleaded.

Stan put his arms around Helter and held him as if he were an injured child. When he spoke next, he sounded as if he was trying to convince himself.

"We'll go to the drugstore," Stan said. "We'll get medicine. We'll put you to sleep and we'll get the bullet out. You'll live. You'll be fine."

Helter's voice cracked. "I want to die. I can't live like this in this horrible place." A spasm of pain shook his frame and his spine arched as he let out a deafening howl. "Stop it! Somebody stop it!"

Stan stared desperately at Pepper and me. "What can we do?"

Pepper was the color of chalk. "I don't know. There's nothing we can do." He shook his head and bit his lower lip. "We should do what he wants us to do."

Stan looked faint. "We can't just kill him. I can't."

Pepper was panting. "I can't either."

"No," I cried. "Let's not talk this way. Do something to help him."

"That's the problem," Stan yelled, still hugging Helter. "We can't help him. No one can."

A bloody hand reached out and touched my hand. Helter screwed his face up at me, his breath coming in burning gasps. He spoke to me as if I was a god.

"Make it end, Roxanne," he whispered.

I held his eyes a moment. What did I see? What he saw in the mirror when he shot at it in terror? Perhaps. Certainly I saw something that had been shattered beyond repair. Maybe that's what Betty Sue really was—a walking wave of destruction. You could not get out of its way. You could only bow before it. I came to a decision.

"Leave us alone," I said flatly.

"What are you going to do, Rox?" Pepper asked.

"He's hurt real bad," Stan said.

"I know," I said and squeezed Helter's hand. "Go now, the two of you. I'll be out in a minute."

They stared at me in amazement. Then Stan eased out from under Helter and let him lay on the floor. Stan stood beside Pepper, staring at Helter, at me. I don't know which frightened the two of them more. They backed away practically holding on to each other, and vanished. I turned back to Helter.

"What a screwed-up day this has been," I said.

He nodded. His breathing had become a bit steadier and he was no longer shaking, but he was still in terrible pain. There was no reason it should go on.

"I wish I hadn't woken up," he gasped.

"I know the feeling." I picked up the revolver,

surprised at its weight. I had never cared for guns. They were only good for one thing, which was a bad thing. Helter watched me as I cocked the hammer. "Was she that strange to be with?" I asked.

He nodded weakly. "She was like a worm. You would hold her, but when you let go you felt like she had slipped inside your guts, and started to grow." He glanced down at his pants and whimpered. "She was bad."

"Why did you go out with her?" I asked.

"Because she would." He coughed. "She would do anything."

"Did you rape her?"

He shook his head, and he was so sorry, it broke my heart. "I don't know what I did. It was one of those nights where I felt her inside my head and I couldn't get her out. That's why I was afraid when Stan started talking about her. She knew how to get inside. She knew all the right doors. I was just trying to get her out." He coughed again. "I guess I did rape her. I wish I had killed her."

"I wish you had, too, Helter," I said gently. I raised the gun to his forehead. "Close your eyes. I'll close mine."

He nodded. "Thank you, Roxanne."

"It's no problem."

I pulled the trigger. I killed him. I never knew I could kill someone. But then I remembered I had gone for an abortion only that morning. Maybe it had prepared me.

I dropped the gun and stood up. I could feel his blood all over me, but I had yet to open my eyes. I turned and walked in the direction where I believed the door was. I was not sure I would find it. Maybe Betty Sue had changed its location, I thought. She knew all the right doors.

I felt like I had just passed through a major door. Now I would find out whether I had taken the wrong one.

CHAPTER XI

THE SUN WAS SAYING GOODBYE TO THE SKY WHEN I stepped outside. The wind blew particles of sand that stung my skin. My hair whipped behind my head and I felt drops of Helter's blood shake loose. I took a deep breath and thought how good it was to be alive. Then I laughed like a sick drunk. I think I was losing my mind. It was about time.

I was in shock. It was as if the bullet had gone through my own brain and out the other side. I felt a part of me that had been good and moral was forever gone.

The guys were standing beneath a tree in front of the gym. Pepper shuddered visibly as I approached. Stan stared at me like he was seeing a stranger.

"Hi," I said.

"Did you do it?" Pepper asked.

"Sure," I said. "Why not? It was probably in the script."

"We have to find the rest of the stories," Stan said.

I laughed again. "Why? Tearing them up didn't do any good. Nothing's going to do any good. Why don't we just go sit in one of the classrooms and write our own stories? Who knows? Maybe Betty Sue will be pleased and give us a passing grade."

"We have to know what's going to happen next," Stan said.

"Nothing will happen next unless we make it happen," I said. "I say we plant ourselves in a field and act like corn stalks. Let the storm pass."

"That might not be a bad idea," Stan said. "But we're not going to do it." He gestured back the way we had come. "We'll get flashlights and look for more pieces of paper."

Pepper stopped him. "Shouldn't we bury Helter first?"

Stan shook his head. "Helter will have to wait."

We got flashlights, fresh batteries. I changed my shirt. I had whole stores to choose from. It was wonderful—a shopper's dream. I left on my bloody pants. They had become a part of me.

We started again near Betty Sue's house and worked our way downwind. We walked unarmed, like good little campers. The task should have been hopeless from the start, but it was amazing how many pieces of notebook paper we collected. By the time we neared the square, we had pocketfuls. Stan made us stop. He tried to put some of them together. More puzzles, I thought. It was now entirely dark, but the lights in the square were still working and we were grateful for small favors.

"What if we don't put them together?" I asked as Stan taped in the beams of our flashlights. "What if they don't work unless we read them?"

Stan glanced up. "I doubt Steve Kinder read his story."

"Which one was he?" Pepper asked.

"The boy who got cancer after he moved away from here," I said. I waved my hand at Stan. "Go ahead."

Stan had been working for maybe ten minutes when he stopped and frowned. "I think we've got only two stories here, not three."

"I hope it's me she left out," Pepper muttered. He looked over at me. "Just kidding."

"I hope she did leave you alone," I told him solemnly, kneeling beside him. In the soft light he was even more handsome than usual. I thought back to our first date then, and put my head back to stare up at the stars. A part of me turned cold and died.

"Do you think there's anyone out here?"

"No one human."

There were no clouds in the sky, no haze, no smoke. And there was no stars either. Betty Sue must have failed to write them in. She probably knew how much I loved them. A strangled cry escaped my lips, and Pepper had to reach over and catch me because I no longer cared if I fell. He cradled me in his arms, and stared into my eyes. Then his own gaze lifted to the sky and he, too, began to shake. I heard Stan's voice.

"We have to believe her now," he said.

I climbed out of Pepper's arms with difficulty and scooted over beside our class genius. "If she can take away the universe," I said. "She can do anything."

Stan seemed beaten. "I have no answers for you."

I touched Stan's knee. "Could she kill us tonight,

and bring us back tomorrow? Could she kill us over and over? Forever?"

Stan put a hand to his head. "I don't think she can bring back the dead."

"Why not?" I asked.

He sat still for a moment, then twitched involuntarily. "Let's see what the stories can tell us."

Stan worked for another few minutes. He could have worked for hours, I wouldn't have cared. I had stopped being aware of time. Who was to say there would be a tomorrow? The sun was only a star, after all, and maybe Betty Sue could have moved it as far away as she wished, into another dimension if she so desired.

Finally Stan Reese had a story for us to read.

It was about him.

SODA RADAR GOES TO SLEEP

Soda Radar was court jester to Queen Beetle. Soda would tell his queen stories while she sat on a magnificent chair and sewed with her needles. She sewed dresses and cloaks, and sometimes they ended up on the fire and turned to smoke. Queen Beetle was wonderful and Soda Radar was sometimes disrespectful. She told him, "Your stories have no rhyme, no sense of time. And that is the worst of crimes." Then she sent Soda into the woods to think of a story that would deliver the goods. She told him he had best get better or she would tickle him with a feather.

Soda picked up a stone, and turned over a bone. He looked at all the things of the woods to make a story, but came no closer to true glory. Then he said to himself, "Queen Beetle is not so smart. I will tell her a story from the past, from a time that has not been marked. She will think it is mine. Then she will treat me kind." He returned to the court of Queen Beetle, and went to her private chamber while she sat sewing with her needles.

"I have brought you a story of wonder," Soda said. "A tale that will ring in your soul like thunder." Then he told her about Salt and Pepper and the plate of late dinner. The story of kids and the end of time and cold winter. Queen Beetle smiled as he spoke, but inside her clasped hands she readied her needles for a poke. Soda did not know this and finished happy, thinking he had presented himself in a tone that was both clear and snappy.

"I can see I kept you from being bored," Soda said. "I am happy you are pleased, and now I want my reward."

Queen Beetle stood and her height was good. She said, "From day one you hovered near me like flies. You sing and dance but really you think of it all as lies. Your story is not new, but old. And I have decided it is time you were sold."

Then Queen Beetle took her needles and grabbed Soda's arm and began to do him great harm. But he cried aloud and said, "Do not do this to me your slave. I apologize and promise never again to misbehave."

Queen Beetle laughed and gave him her needle. "Poke yourself so that you bleed," she said. "Then I will take what is left of you, and give it to someone who is in need."

Then Soda took her needle and stuck it hard into his heart. His blood poured onto the floor, and after some time he had to close his eyes, and inside it grew dark.

"Cheery," I said.

"I love the upbeat endings," Pepper agreed. He patted Stan on the back. "None of it has to happen."

But Stan was ashen. "I used to think of her as my queen," he whispered.

"Why?" I asked.

"Because she was so powerful," he said.

"And you visited her whenever she wanted you to?" I asked.

He nodded miserably. "I had no choice."

"That witch," I said.

Stan stood. "Excuse me. I have to get something from the drugstore."

I jumped up. "What?"

"I have a headache," he said. "I need some aspirin."

"We'll go with you," I said.

He stopped us. "It's not necessary. I'll be back in a couple of minutes." He handed us the remainder of his notebook scraps. "See if you can piece together the final story."

It was my turn to stop him. "You're OK, aren't you?" I asked.

He smiled. Such a nice guy. The best really, of all of us. "Sure," he said.

"Don't go picking up any needles," I said. "I'm serious."

He nodded, but there was no life to the gesture. "I understand."

Stan slowly walked away in the direction of the drugstore, the one beside the bank. Just before going inside he stopped at a newspaper rack. He fished inside his pocket for change and bought himself a paper. Then he went inside the drugstore.

"I think I should go with him," I fretted to Pepper.

"You might want to stay with me," Pepper said. He was already on the ground, fiddling with the scraps Stan had left behind. The wind was hassling his efforts. There was sand in his hair and I brushed it out.

"Why do you need me now?" I asked.

He glanced at me. "Because, in case you didn't notice, I was mentioned in Stan's story. And I can already see that this last story's got my name all over it."

"Oh."

He paused. "Why do you hate me, Rox?"

I was annoyed. "I don't hate you. Why do you say something stupid like that?"

"You haven't been particularly nice to me today."

"Well, I'm sorry, it has been a kind of bad day." I popped my hands on my hips, a gesture I never normally used. "You haven't been nice to me either."

Pepper tried to lean over to touch me, but I was standing just out of reach. "What is it?" he asked.

"Why don't you tell me?"

"Tell you what?"

"About your relationship with Betty Sue for one thing," I said. "I know you had one. Your name is all over her burnt diary."

He was obviously worried, which did wonders for my confidence in him. "What did it say?" he asked.

"Does it matter? I want to know what *you* have to say." I took a step closer. "We used to tell each other everything, Pepper. Tell me now about her. I don't know how much longer we'll have to talk."

He stared at his feet, sitting perfectly still for a minute. He closed his eyes, keeping his hands pressed on top of the scraps of the last story.

"I went out with her a few times," he said finally. "She had a mystery about her that I found fascinating. But we didn't do anything interesting." He opened his eyes and shrugged. "We went to a couple of movies, ate dinner a few times."

"Did you kiss her?"

He hesitated. "Yes."

"Did you have sex with her?"

He faced me straight on, his dark eyes wide. "No, Rox."

"Did you go out with her after you went out with me?"

"No." He raised his hand. "I swear to God I didn't."

I took a deep breath. The world had come to an end. The stars had been vanquished. Yet I felt so relieved. I leaned down and gave him a tight hug. "You sure know how to pick 'em," I said.

"Are you referring to yourself or to her?" he asked.

I let him go and stood straight. "Both." I glanced at the drugstore. "Stay here a second and put the rest of the story together. I want to check on Stan."

Pepper started to get up. "Don't you want me to come with you?"

Once more I was breaking the cardinal rule of real life horror. But I answered without hesitating. "No."

I passed the newspaper stand as I approached the drugstore. The *Salem Herald*—circulation four thousand and fifteen, if something was happening in town. The bin was empty. I wondered if Stan had taken the last copy. I opened the door to the drugstore and went inside.

The lights were out. Stan had not bothered to turn them on. But enough illumination came in from the square lamps to keep me from bumping into things. Stan sat on the counter near the front, his legs dangling down, leaning back on his arms. One page of the newspaper rested on his lap.

"Hi," he said softly.

"How's the headache?" I asked.

"Better."

"Did you take something?"

"Yeah."

"Good." I sat down on the floor at his feet, looking up at him in the silent dimness. He appeared more at ease than he had a few minutes earlier, and that made me relax. "So, what's new in the news?" I asked.

He nodded with his head for me to take the paper

off his lap. Apparently he was too comfortable the way he was sitting to move.

"It's only the first page," he said.

"Is it today's paper?" I asked, reaching out for it.

"Tomorrow's."

I froze as I touched the paper, afraid to take it. "How's that?"

"It has tomorrow's news in it," Stan said.

"Have you read it?"

"Yes."

"Is it bad?"

"Yes."

I sat back on my butt. I had the single sheet in my hand—just the one. I turned it over without reading the headlines. Blank. Betty Sue had not wanted to waste ink. I turned to the front. The headlines. Destiny.

TRAGEDY STRIKES FIVE LOCAL TEENS

Beneath the caption were five small pictures. Senior pictures that would be in the yearbook when it came out in a month or so. Leslie's picture. Helter's and Pepper's and Stan's. Mine, too—I wasn't smiling as the others were.

"Should I read the article?" I asked.

"There's only the first half of it," Stan said. "But it's interesting."

"Interesting," I muttered. I began to read.

Five Salem teens died yesterday: Leslie Belle, Helter Skater, Stan Reese, Paul Pointzel, and

Roxanne Wells. Each death appears to be an isolated incident, unconnected to the others. But local authorities are not dismissing the possibility of a "group suicide pact," although not all the deaths were apparent suicides.

Leslie Belle died in her garage at approximately two in the afternoon when the gas tank of her car exploded. Her parents were out at the time. It appears Leslie was trying to pour extra gasoline into her tank from a can of fuel her father reserved for supplying his lawnmower. There is speculation that she had a cigarette in her mouth at the time of the incident, although her parents deny that she smoked. It is thought that she died instantly. Nobody else was injured in the explosion.

Helter Skater died at Salem High when he either intentionally or accidentally shot himself in the groin and the head with a Colt .45 revolver. His body was found in the girls' shower room Saturday evening. Authorities don't know how he came to be there.

Stan Reese's body was found at approximately ten last night in his bed. His parents were home at the time, but didn't know there was any problem with their son. Police are saying Stan was a probable suicide because both his wrists had been slit, but there was no note, as is usual with suicides. His parents felt that Stan was still distraught over the suicide of Betty Sue McCormick, who only four weeks earlier doused herself with gasoline and lit herself on fire.

The fourth victim to be found was Paul Pointzel, who died at—(*Please Turn to Page Three:* TRAGEDY).

"She would end it just there," I complained.

"I don't know," Stan said softly. "Maybe she didn't write it. Maybe it's the way it will be written."

I set aside the page. Actually, I dropped it, and it floated slowly to the floor. "So we know the truth at last. We're dead. We don't have to worry anymore. It's over."

I felt like crying right then, but my tears were used up. Did I believe my own words? I hoped not. Death couldn't feel this awful, I thought, not if there was a God. But what if there wasn't? What if the soul did survive for eternity, but in a careless chasm where no divine will reigned supreme? That truly would be hell. We would be forever at the mercy of Betty Sue's wicked games.

"Maybe we're not dead," Stan said. "And not alive. Maybe we're somewhere in between."

"Is that possible?"

"I don't know."

I forced a chuckle. "One thing for sure, I'm not letting you go near your bedroom."

He yawned. "That's too bad. I feel like a nap right now."

I stood up and stretched. "Pepper's trying to piece together the other story. Maybe we should get back to him."

"Would it be OK if we sat here a little longer?" he asked.

He sounded so sad, I didn't have the heart to say no. I sat back down. "Sure. Whatever you want. Do you have any new ideas on what we should do next?"

"Explore the truth," he said.

"What do you mean? What truth?"

He sighed and let his head roll back on his neck. His arms were still behind him, supporting him. He was breathing hard, but I figured it was because the stillness inside the drugstore was claustrophobic. Of course so was the night air outside, beneath the starless sky.

"Betty Sue called me over to her house the last day of her life," Stan said in a dreamy voice. "It was not one of those times when I felt I had to go see her. Still, I wanted to say no to her. She sounded strange, even for her. But she said I had to come. She needed my help."

"What was her problem?" I asked.

Stan grimaced in the shadows. "She was pregnant. She told me the minute I walked in her bedroom. She said she had to get rid of the baby and she had to do it that day."

"Do you know who the father was?"

Stan thought a moment. "No."

"Did the father know she was pregnant?"

"I think so."

"Go on," I said.

Stan's head came forward and hung over slightly. He seemed weary to the bone. His breathing was definitely labored. "This is the thing I didn't want to tell you about," he said. "She was playing with me. Maybe she was already playing with all of us."

"She wasn't really pregnant?"

He shook his head. "She was and she wasn't. She had already started to get rid of the baby—at least that's what she said."

Even before I asked, and he answered, I felt sick to my stomach. "What do you mean?" I whispered.

Stan sighed. "I don't know the gory details, thank God. But she said she had done something to her insides. When I got there she was hemorrhaging internally. She looked fine, at first, but then she told me what was happening. Then I saw stains on her—I don't even want to say it. I believe she was telling me the truth. She wouldn't let me take her to the hospital. She wasn't scared. Like I told you earlier, she was happy. She told me she had an exciting evening planned."

I pressed my hands to my ears. "I can't listen to this."

Stan was sympathetic. "I understand. I begged her to let me help her, but she refused. She said she knew how to take care of herself. She said she was going to make herself invincible, so that nothing could ever hurt her again. Then she would come back in style."

"Come back?"

"Spooky, yeah. But first she said she had to take care of some unfinished business. She wanted me to get her a few things."

"What kind of things?"

"Pictures of Helter and Leslie and Pepper and you. She also wanted a picture of me."

"She needed them to make voodoo dolls?" I asked.

"I never thought of it that way. Yeah, in a sense. Her stories are like those dolls."

"Why did she want *you* to get the pictures?" I asked.

"I was probably her only friend. And I was on the yearbook staff. It was easy for me to obtain the pictures. I got her copies of the ones you just saw on the front page of the newspaper."

"Why did you do it?" I asked.

"I didn't know she was planning next month's news." He shrugged. "I don't know if I had a choice in the matter."

"Why didn't she get them herself?"

"That's an interesting question. I believe she wanted me to know what she was up to so that when we ended up here—wherever we are—I would suspect that she had something to do with it."

"Did she say anything else that led you to believe she could work such a major miracle?"

"Two things. She told me just before I left that her butterfly jar could be any size she wanted it to be." He sat up straighter, and it was a major effort. He was dozing as he spoke. "That's why I didn't want you to try to leave town. I didn't think you'd be able to."

"You thought we'd run into a glass wall?"

"Something like that." He coughed. "All day long we've been flying in tiny circles. And dying." He added, "It's been hot today."

"What was the other thing she said?" I asked.

He raised his head as if it weighed a ton, and met my eyes. "You went to Foster this morning to get an abortion, didn't you?"

I was shocked that he'd know. "Did Pepper—"

"No," he interrupted. "I knew because she told me that there would be another like her, and that she'd use this other to screw tight the lid on her jar."

"What does that mean?"

"Since we're talking about Betty Sue, I'd venture to say she needed you and your situation as an important ingredient in her curse."

"But I didn't get an abortion. I couldn't go through with it and got up and left in the middle."

Stan's head jerked at the remark. "In the middle?"

"Before the procedure got started." I clasped at my abdomen. All day long I had had no ill effects from what the doctor had done to me. I felt safe that I had changed my mind in plenty of time. Yet now, ever so faintly, I felt a cold liquidy sensation in my guts. It crept from the right to the left, like an icy finger across my intestines.

I shook it off. It was probably just Stan's story, I reasoned. It was enough to make anybody's stomach turn.

"I didn't mean to pry into your private business," Stan said.

"No problem. Did you see her again after you left to get the pictures?"

"No. She didn't want to see me. She wanted me to get the pictures, put them in an envelope, and slide them under her bedroom door. And that's what I did."

"How come you didn't tell Betty Sue's mother what was wrong?"

"She wasn't around."

"You should have told someone."

Stan gestured helplessly. "She didn't want me to."

"Was Betty Sue in her room when you returned with the pictures?"

"Yes. I called to her, but she didn't answer. I think she was writing. Probably these stories." Stan raised his head once more, and I was surprised to see tears streaming down his cheeks. "Oh, God," he whispered.

"Stan?"

He sniffed. "You know everyone thought I was pretty smart. I was a nerd but I had respect. People didn't make fun of me. They liked me, and I liked them. My life was pretty good."

"It was a great life."

Stan shook his head sadly. "It couldn't be great because deep down inside I was a coward. I knew what was right and I knew what was wrong. I knew everything connected with Betty Sue was wrong. But I did what she said because I was afraid of her." His voice cracked. "I should never have brought her those pictures."

"It wasn't your fault." I got up and stepped to his side. "Come on, let's get out of this drugstore. It's got bad vibes. Let's go see Pepper. The night's young. We'll think of something to do. It'll be OK."

Stan refused to budge. "I can't go," he mumbled.

"Come on," I said, tugging at his arm. "We'll make a plan. We'll . . ."

I stopped. I had stepped into a dark puddle. It was coming from the back of the counter, through the druggist's walkway. A whiff of a sickly copper odor touched my nostrils and stabbed right into my heart. I leaned around where Stan sat and saw that the puddle

144

ormed from twin trickles pouring off the counter.
And following the course back a bit further, I realized
hat Stan had slit his wrists and was bleeding to death
ight now.

"Stan, no," I moaned.

"I'm sorry," he whispered as he sagged into my
arms. I caught him before he could fall. He was cold to
he touch. He continued to weep. "I had to do what
she said."

"But why?" I cried.

"I don't know why. It's always been this way." He
coughed some more, and buried his face in my chest. I
believe I felt his heart flutter in his chest. It was
probably low on blood to pump. It was amazing Stan
was even conscious. The puddle soaked the entire
space behind the counter. "I wanted to save you and
Pepper from her," he said pitifully.

I hugged him tight. "You did your best." I kissed the
side of his face. "Can't we try to stop the bleeding?"

"It's too late." He sat back slightly, wrapping his
bleeding arms around him, shivering. "I'm so cold."

"Why is she doing this to you? You were her
friend."

"Maybe that made me her worst enemy. I was the
only one who knew her secrets and still liked her. I
had to be gotten rid of."

I ran my hand through his hair. "Is there anything I
can do for you?"

He nodded. "Put me in my bed when I'm gone."

I began to cry. "Then it will be just like the paper.
Then she will have won everything."

He cried with me. "She has won."

"No! I won't let her!" I grabbed his shoulders and he shook in my hands like a rag doll. "You can't die yet! You have to tell me how to stop her!"

But I had apparently waited too long for my emotional plea. Stan tried to speak but collapsed in my arms. I laid him back on the counter. He gasped for air. His skin was white as marble. The vampiress had claimed another victim, damn her to the deepest hell. He gestured me closer. I pressed my ear to his lips to catch his last words. He smiled weakly.

"I always had a crush on you," he said. "I'm glad you passed your math class."

I buried my face in his chest. "I always had a crush on you, Stan."

But I don't know if he heard me. He didn't answer, and when I sat back up, his eyes were open, staring at a distant ceiling that covered the invisible stars. I closed his eyes for him and folded his arms across his chest.

"Goodbye, old friend," I said.

CHAPTER XII

PEPPER TOOK THE NEWS HARD. CAN'T SAY I BLAMED HIM. Once there were five and now there were two. I couldn't bear to think which one of us would go next.

"We have to get out of here," Pepper said desperately.

"I don't know if we can," I said, thinking of the glass jar. Pepper held me by my shoulders. He looked ten years older than he had that morning. I hadn't told him about the newspaper. I suppose I didn't want to worry him.

"We can't stay here," he said. "Her power may not extend beyond the limits of the city."

I nodded. I had no strength left to argue. "We can leave as soon as we move Stan's body to his bedroom."

"Forget it!" Pepper said, letting go of me. "Every second we stay here is dangerous. Stan's dead. We can't help him."

I turned toward the drugstore. "It was his last wish. I'm going to move him to his bed with or without your help."

Pepper grabbed me from behind. I had never seen

such fear, and I had seen a lot of it that very day. "We have to leave *now*. I read the last story."

"What did it say?" I asked. Stupid question. He pulled a handful of paper scraps from his pocket.

"It says that I'm going to die," he replied, thrusting the mutilated story in my face. I sat down and put it together. Another voodoo doll.

SALT AND PEPPER FOR SUPPER

Salt and Pepper were a happy couple. They laughed and kissed, and when they were apart it was as if something was amiss. But they were only spices. All they had were flavor and a few miserable vices.

It came to pass one day that Salt and Pepper met Fat Freddy. He said to them, "I will take you to my queen. Are you keen?" Salt said, "I do not know her name. I do not know if the one I think of is the same." But Pepper said, "I know this great queen. I have heard she never gets mean." So Fat Freddy took Salt and Pepper to meet Queen Beetle, and they found her sewing in her secret chamber with her needles.

Queen Beetle said, "I know this Pepper. He kissed me once but then he left and never wrote me a letter." Then Pepper was afraid and clung tight to Salt. Pepper was so afraid he would not tell Salt it was all his fault. But it was time for Queen Beetle's dinner, and because she was never rude, she invited them to stay. Salt and Pepper said fine, thinking they were hungry and might dine. But they did not know Queen Beetle's hate, and when they looked away she snatched them both and set them on her plate.

The Queen said, "Do not scream, or I will certainly cut you like a bean." But Salt protested, "Why are you doing this, why do you hate?" To which Queen Beetle laughed. "It is not simply hate. It is much more honorable. It is fate."

Then Queen Beetle picked up her knife and fork, and reached for her bottled wine and pulled the cork. "A toast!" Queen Beetle exclaimed. "For the flavor Salt and Pepper give to my roast!" Then Queen Beetle stretched out with her knife and fork, and Salt was so angry at Pepper that she pushed him onto the Queen's pork. There Pepper caught the Queen's fork, and it pierced his chest, and he died like a foolish dork.

"Lovely," I said. I looked up at Pepper from the curb where I was sitting and reading. The wind howled. The sand blew. Our flashlights rocked. Such a scene, this cruel night. "Was this all your fault?" I asked.

"What are you talking about?" Pepper asked.

I thought of the story Stan had told me. Betty Sue's last day. "Never mind," I said flatly.

Pepper knelt anxiously at my side. "You're not angry at me, are you?"

I touched his face. "No."

He glanced down at the story. "Please don't get angry at me."

I let go of the scraps of paper, and the wind carried them off into the night. "I understand," I said.

We took care of Stan. We put him in the backseat of my car and drove to his house. We carried him into his bedroom and eased him under the blankets. I wanted to bandage his wrists, but Pepper wouldn't let me. I left the light on in the bedroom. I turned in the doorway and peeked at him one last time.

"At least he looks peaceful now," I said to Pepper.

"The dead always do," Pepper muttered.

I thought of Helter, what was left of his head. "I don't know about that."

Then we were outside again, in the dark windy part of Betty Sue's universe. My car had gas in it—we had got five bucks in it that morning at the deserted station. We took Highway 37 out of town, the same road we had taken to Foster for the abortion. But this time we headed north on it. I insisted on it. Pepper didn't mind. He talked as we drove.

"We'll get to L.A. tomorrow morning," he said. "We'll go straight to the beach. We can be walking beside the water when the sun comes up."

"That sounds wonderful." I stared out the window as Salem shrank behind us. The wind was worse than I could remember all day. Pepper had to fight to keep the car moving in a straight line. We were being sandblasted. By the time we'd reach the other end of the desert, there wouldn't be a speck of paint left on the exterior.

"You know it's possible there might be other people in L.A.," he said. "I respect the things Stan said. I'm sure Betty Sue was a weird chick. No one can argue with that. But Stan might have taken the thing with her too far. We might find people everywhere."

"I hope you're right." Of course I didn't believe a word of it. But if the talk made Pepper feel better, then I wasn't going to argue with him. The front of the car swerved dangerously in a strong gust. "We should slow down."

"I'm only doing forty-five," Pepper said.

"Do thirty-five."

Pepper nodded and slowed. "At least in L.A. we won't have to worry about affordable housing. We'll be able to stay anywhere we like." He glanced over at me. "Where would you like to stay?"

"Beverly Hills."

"Why there?"

"It sounds rich," I said.

"How about Malibu? It's rich, too, and it's by the ocean."

"Malibu would be fine with me."

"We could go see all the sights," Pepper said. "It might even be better that everyone's gone. We won't have to wait in any lines. Hey, we could go to Disneyland! We'll have the whole park to ourselves. Won't that be a trip?"

"How will we get the rides to work?"

"It can't be that hard to turn them on. We'll probably just have to push a button or something."

I nodded, enjoying the fantasy. It was all we had left. The wind was getting stronger and stronger, coming at us straight on now. Pepper had to keep the gas floored to maintain a meager speed.

"I want to go on Space Mountain first," I said.

"You know the name of the actual rides?" he asked.

"I know lots of them. There's Space Mountain, Pirates of the Caribbean, Thunder Mountain, and the Haunted Mansion."

Pepper laughed. "Maybe we could skip the Haunted Mansion."

I laughed, too. "Yeah. We have Salem for that."

Pepper shook his head. "Can you believe the stuff that happened to us today?"

"Nope. I hope when I wake up tomorrow it's all forgotten."

"So you think we might just be dreaming?"

The car swerved again harshly. "Careful!" I cried.

"I am being careful." Pepper leaned forward and tried to peer through the sandstorm. Our visibility was almost nonexistent. Our speed was down to maybe ten miles an hour. "This is unreal," he muttered.

"Can you see?" I asked anxiously.

"I see what you see."

"Maybe we should try to leave tomorrow."

"No," he snapped.

The noise of the sand rained in my ears like a meteor storm in outer space. "But if we crash, what good will it do us?"

He was adamant. "We're not going back. We'll die if we go back."

Ten minutes went by. In that time we didn't talk about Disneyland or Beverly Hills. We sat in silence, because we both realized what was happening. The power of the wind was growing in direct proportion to our distance from Salem. Pepper had the accelerator floored and we were barely creeping forward. Outside the windshield was a wall of moving brown dust.

"We're beginning to overheat," Pepper said.

"Our glass jar," I whispered.

"What?" Pepper yelled over the racket.

"We have to go back."

He shook his head. "No!"

"Then just stop the car and we'll sit here." I grabbed his arm. "Pepper, it's no use!"

He took his foot off the gas and stopped the car. We sat for a minute in the loud darkness. It was ironic—all day I prayed for the silence to lift, and now that I had noise, it was driving me crazy.

"We can't just sit here," Pepper said finally.

"Turn around."

He touched my knee. "You won't get mad at me if we go back?"

"Why would I get mad? I'm the one who said we have to go back."

He let go of my leg. "I just wanted to get that straight."

We turned around with difficulty, but once we were pointed toward Salem we could have returned without any gas. The wind pushed the car happily along, until the town became visible. That's when the storm—no big surprise here—suddenly eased. As we crossed the city limits a feeling of despair swept over me, like that of falling into a bottomless well, where no matter how long you dropped, you never hit bottom. Never feel the icy black water seep into your black heart. Still, you knew it was there for you—eventually. Like oblivion. Death.

Pepper looked over at me. "Where would you like to spend the night?" he asked.

I smiled sadly. "Disneyland Hotel."

"Where else?"

"Your place," I said.

But who spoke? Who made us choose that place? I believe it was *her*.

Pepper's house stood silent and black at the edge of town. We parked in the driveway but we didn't go inside. By unspoken agreement we took each other's hands and walked to the barn. The cozy hay. Our love nest. God, that night seemed like a million years ago.

Indeed, suddenly, it seemed as if it had never happened. At least not to me. It was as if Pepper had been holding another girl that night, when he was supposed to be holding me.

Many things came clear to me as we stepped inside. They came clear to me in darkness.

Yes, it's true, something swept over me all right. Perhaps the wind brought it. I cannot explain the power of it except to say it was profoundly subtle. So subtle I didn't know at the time it wasn't of my own making. I experienced a clarity of a cruel kind.

Pepper lit a lantern and hung it on a brown wooden beam. I sat in the loft of hay and lazily swung my legs. Up and down, back and forth. I was thinking. I wished I could stop. Our thoughts had been our enemies all day. If we'd just decided to lie down and take a long nap when we met at the ice-cream parlor, we would have all been alive still. But perhaps that was not our fate. Pepper sat beside me and put his arm around my shoulder.

"What's the matter?" he asked.

"Nothing."

"You look sad?" he said.

"I am. Very sad."

He nodded. "At least we're together."

I looked at him. The blue green prairie in his eyes. The sunshine in his mouth. My Pepper. I looked at a stranger.

"Did you sleep with Betty Sue?" I asked.

He blinked. "No."

I took his arm off my shoulder and stood, staring down at him. "Did you have sex with her?" I demanded.

He got up also, and stood in front of me, up on the loft. On the soft hay in the soft light of the warm lantern. "No," he said.

I chewed on my lower lip. I tasted blood. It tasted like it had been mingled and polluted with another's blood. That was true in a sense, I thought. I was carrying Pepper's child. What blood would pump in the veins of that child? It made no difference to me right then that the fetus hadn't even grown a heart yet. I felt as if I was no different from the undeveloped baby. Suddenly my heart was not working. All I could do was think of Pepper in the arms of Betty Sue, both of them naked, both of them having fun. My boyfriend. My true love. Honest to God, if I hadn't loved him so much it couldn't have hurt so much. But that is, I believe, why God gave us love. So that we could feel pain. It made us that much more mortal. It made us that much less than God. In the end, all love did was bring pain to me. Goddamn the way things are, I thought.

I took a step closer to Pepper. "You're lying to me."

He shook his head quickly. "No, Rox. I . . ."

"You're lying to me!" I screamed. "You screwed her! You got her pregnant!"

Pepper froze. The life simply fell out of his face. Then he raised his hands to cover his face. And I was glad. I didn't want to have to look at him. It disgusted me when he began to weep.

"I'm sorry," he moaned. "I didn't want to tell you because I didn't want to hurt you." He shrugged. No, he shook. He trembled as if the blood in his veins had become ice. "It was just something that happened. I didn't plan it. I didn't care for her at all."

I pulled his hands down from his face. I screwed my face up into his and breathed fire on his shame. "All I want to know," I said with deadly calm, "is whether you screwed her before or after you screwed me? Tell me the truth. Don't lie to me. If you lie to me, I'll get angry. And we both know how dangerous that can be."

He twitched. "Before."

I sucked in a breath and slowly reached up and grabbed him by the collar. "And after?" I asked.

He twitched again and swallowed hard. "Just once," he said.

I let him go. "I see," I said.

Then I shoved him backward. Not all that hard. But he fell, I watched him fall over the wooden railing, off the loft, and onto the soft hay below. No big deal. I had done almost the same thing the night we made love. But I should have remembered that night better. It hadn't been that long ago, that close call. I should have at least remembered Betty Sue's story. Queen Beetle and her fork digging into her peppery pork.

The pitchfork was in the hay. It was hidden, just barely, beneath the light brown straw. Worst of all, it was pointed up. Pepper landed on it on his back and in an instant all six blades pierced his chest. I saw them pop out the front. Red steel going through the cotton shirt I had bought for his birthday. Blood mushroomed over his front. I saw him open his mouth and try to scream but blood poured from around his teeth and drowned him out. God, there was so much blood.

"Pepper," I said as I stared down at him from the loft. I didn't know what else to say. I couldn't very well say I was sorry, although suddenly I was more sorry than I had ever been in my life. The power of the spell had been broken, at last. I understood that's what my anger had been. Leslie had taken up smoking because she was under a spell. Helter had fired repeatedly into his own reflection because the curse was working on his mind. Stan had slit his wrists open because she had told him to. In my own way, I had done what I was told.

Pepper gagged.

I climbed down from the loft and knelt by his side. Betty Sue had lined us all up and now she was almost through knocking us down. This was the third time in one day I had knelt beside a dying friend. It wasn't getting any easier—oh no. I looked at him, struggling like a pinned butterfly trying to free itself of a painful needle, and I could not understand. I just refused to understand such horror. I thought that if I did I would know the universe's worst secret.

What a joke—I knew it already.

No matter how bad things got, they could always get worse.

"Pepper," I said and took his trembling hand. He couldn't lay still, couldn't lay back. The damn thing had him propped up in severe discomfort. I watched the red liquid soak down from each individual gleaming knife. It wouldn't be long, I thought. Pepper looked over at me like a sad boy who had lost his mommy. I would have yanked the pitchfork from his back and thrust it through my own chest if it would have eased his sorrow the tiniest bit. But it would have done nothing so I did nothing. "I'm sorry," I said.

"Rox," he gasped.

I leaned closer, placing his hand on my heart. "Yes?"

"I'm sorry, too," he whispered. "You were . . . first. Only . . . one."

I nodded. I understood. He hadn't lied to me, not really. "You were my first and only."

He glanced down at the red blades protruding from his chest. Blood trickled out the side of his mouth. "No escape," he moaned.

I put my free hand on his forehead. He felt warm, and for a second I worried he was catching something. Silly me. I had always wanted to take care of him. Always and forever.

"There is an escape," I said. "We've already taken it. We escaped when we fell in love at the reservoir. The spaceships came for us and carried us away up to the stars." I kissed his face. "I'll be with you soon, sweetie. We'll go to the stars together." I began to cry. I didn't want to. I wanted to be strong for him, as he had been strong for me these last few months. I pressed a bloody hand to my eyes, but my tears just ran red and wouldn't stop. All the things that had happened to me so far—they were nothing compared to this. They were like the dream, and this was the painful reality. My life hadn't really started until Pepper had entered it. Now I felt my life ending, even before Betty Sue could get her hands on me. "Wait for me," I cried. "Please?"

He looked at me with exhausted eyes. "Rox . . . love you."

I nodded vigorously, sobbing uncontrollably. "Yes, Pepper. I love you, too." I hugged him, my arms going around him and the metal prongs. I think it was all right to squeeze him tight. I had done it before. I used to squeeze him so hard I'd pretend I was squeezing his soul into my soul. But right then I didn't have to pretend. I felt it was real this time. His soul, his love—so warm, so sweet, so soft—it was like I could touch it directly. All of Betty Sue's lies had washed off me. Thank God I'd had a chance to love this guy, I thought. It had made all the pain worthwhile.

"Thank God," I said, opening my eyes and seeing his eyes closed. His pain was over. He was dead. "Thank God," I repeated.

Chapter XIII

I BURIED HIM IN THE HAY. THERE WAS ONLY ONE HARD part—pulling the pitchfork out of his back. I folded his arms across his chest as I had Stan's. And like Stan, Pepper also looked peaceful.

Then I went for a long walk through the night. The lights had finally failed and the darkness was irrevocable. I walked in Stan's prophetic dream. Yet I never turned to see if I was being followed. I didn't care if I was. My pain and sorrow were so great I was shattered. In a way I was happy the streets were deserted, and that I had no one I had to talk to. The town's emptiness fit my soul. Both were black and filled with agony.

I ended up at Betty Sue's house. Perhaps it was because it was where it had all begun. I felt no special danger. There was no one left to kill me. I wasn't going to arm myself. I wasn't going to smoke around a gasoline pump. I went inside and sat at Betty Sue's desk. There were pen and paper in her desk drawer. And a candle and a match. I lit the candle and opened the window wide so I could feel the wind and sand on

160

my face and arms. Outside I could barely see the street. The sand was sweeping Salem away. I picked up the pen and began to write.

'Cause there was nothing else to do.

I sit alone in a dead world. The wind blows, hot and dry and the dust gathers like particles of memory waiting to be swept away . . .

So I wrote this story, and now it is done. I don't know if anyone will ever find it and read it. I don't know if I care. I just hope that Betty Sue is really dead, and never returns to the land of the living. If she does return, I don't know what could stop her.

My hand is tired. I wish to put my pen down and rest. But I don't dare close my eyes. I don't know what I'd awaken to—if anything. I suppose she could make it so that I die in my sleep.

What is that? I hear a sound. It must be the wind. Yet it doesn't sound like the wind.

It sounds like footsteps. Approaching. Oh, God.

Someone is opening the front door of Betty Sue's house.

She stands in the doorway of her bedroom and stares in at me. She hasn't spoken, but has indicated that I am to keep writing. She is taller than I remember, but then I notice her high black boots. Her coat is long and dark, made of soft leather—it is really more of a cape. Her incredible red hair shines like fire. Her lips are almost as red, set in a line that I cannot fathom. She is amused by me, that much is clear, but she also seems rather melancholy. There is no mistaking the power that radiates from her. This is her place and she knows it.

She approaches and sits on the bed.

"Write as I speak," she says. "Record everything."

"All right," I say. I write down the words. Her green eyes follow me closely. That is another thing we have in common, besides red hair. I could stare in a mirror and see her eyes. Except hers are deeper than mine, and colder.

"Is there anything you want to ask me?" she asks.

"Yes," I say.

"Go ahead."

"Are we dead?"

The question brings a smile to her lips. Her face is so pale, I fear the smile will crack it. But it doesn't. Perhaps Betty Sue can still feel joy. I don't know.

"We are born dead," she says. "It is just a matter of time before we realize it." She touches her belly. "The rare one realizes it even before emerging from the womb."

"I don't understand?"

"I was the one in your womb. I came back for you. You were pregnant with me." She pauses and her smile shrinks. "Mother."

"You came back to kill me?" I ask.

"Yes. But to do that, you had to kill me first."

"I had to decide to have an abortion?"

"Yes. You had a choice not to. Your choice opened the door."

"And sealed tight the lid?"

"Yes," she says.

"But I didn't have the abortion. I stopped it."

"Did you?"

Her question brings ice to my guts. "Yes. I know I topped it."

She does not want to argue the point. "Why?"

"I thought of you," I say. "What a waste it was that you threw your life away. It made me change my mind."

"You thought of me because I was with you then."

"Why do you want to kill me? What did I ever do to you?"

She pauses. She has to think and that scares me. Her thoughts are dangerous. "How many times have you been in love?"

"Once," I say.

"Would you believe I could be in love?" she asks.

"No."

My answer does not offend her. She lowers her head. Her smile is now entirely gone. "I loved Pepper," she says.

"Why?"

She shrugs. "Why did you love him, Roxanne?"

I shiver as she says my name. I know she can curse it just by speaking it out loud. She does not need her pen and paper. "I don't know."

She nods. "It is that way with the best of things, and the worst of things." She gestures around us, to the wind and the sand, the starless sky. "This is all a mystery."

"Even to you?"

She chuckles softly. "Not so much to me."

"Who the hell are you? *What* are you?"

She sits still, her back straight. "I am a storyteller."

She looks out the window at the black night. "God is a storyteller."

"We've been calling you a witch all day. Are you a witch?"

"I am human. But a human can be many things. A human can be a witch. A sorcerer. A saint. A god."

"What are you to me, right now?"

"I told you. Your child." She pauses again. "You made me who I am."

"How? What did I do?"

A shade of sorrow returns to her face. "I went to visit Pepper the night you two were in the barn. I saw you in each others arms."

I have to swallow. "I didn't know."

She takes a deep breath and lets it out slowly. "I think I lost my mind right then. I felt such pain." She looks at me. "You felt that same pain just before you pushed him onto my fork, and afterward." She grins suddenly. "And that's how you made this situation. Do you understand?"

"No."

She gestures again to our empty surroundings. "What would this world be if one child who was born had never been born? Would it be the same world?"

"It would be pretty much the same, I would think, unless the kid was supposed to be president or something important."

Betty Sue speaks strongly. "No. That's not true. That is the mystery. It would not be the same at all. It would be nothing." She pauses and points to her papers and pens. "This world belongs to me alone. It would have been nothing if I had not been born. I sat here and created it. *I* wrote your story. I let you finish it. All my thoughts of you and Helter and Pepper and Stan and Leslie—they were inside my head. I could make them any way I wanted. I could make *you* any way I wanted."

"That wasn't true until today."

She nods. "I had to capture you in my jar." She speaks seriously. "I am the author. I am the storyteller. I am all that there is."

I am offended. "But you're not God?"

She throws her head back and laughs. "Maybe I am. Or maybe I am the devil. What's the difference to someone like me?" Then she shakes her arm slightly and suddenly, like magic, there is a long silver knitting needle in her right hand. She holds it up to the quivering candle. The sharp point glistens like a deadly star.

"Queen Beetle," I say, and I am so scared.

She nods. "You changed your mind too late, Roxanne."

"No." I clasp my abdomen. Inside the cold aches. "No."

"Yes." She leans toward me, her needle in her hand. "The procedure was already underway. Now you are bleeding. You are hemorrhaging. The doctor is worried. He fears he is about to lose you. And he is right."

"That's not true," I cry. But the cold in my guts is getting worse. It spreads like an evil flame from a black abyss. My internal organs shudder. I am having trouble breathing. It is a strain to keep writing. But I fear if I stop writing, my story will be over. She will poke me with her needle. She nods as I think this.

"If you set down the pen," she says. "I will stab you in the belly."

"But I can't keep writing," I protest.

She wets her lower lip with her tongue. "That is the difference between you and me. You had only one story to tell." She stops and grins once more. "I have millions."

"No!" I cry.

She doesn't wait for me to drop the pen. She takes me by surprise. She stabs me with her needle. It goes through my shirt, deep into my belly, into my child. Blood gushes around the wound. I feel the cold inside my heart, the pain. It is a numbing pain, and it spreads. The outside wind begins to die down. I no longer feel the sand on my face. The candle flickers; the room grows dark. I have to put down my pen. The last thing I see is Betty Sue's green eyes, looking at me. There is cruelty in them, and compassion. I don't know which is worse.

Suddenly I am very tired.

PAUL POINTZEL, BETTER KNOWN AS PEPPER, SAT IN THE waiting room of the clinic with the mean nurse and a copy of *People* magazine. The nurse wouldn't talk to him or look at him. She obviously hated all the men who brought in their knocked-up women. The *People* magazine was ancient; several of the celebrities who babbled in the pages about how cool they were now that they had kicked drugs and booze were now appearing on game shows trying to earn extra bucks. Pepper hoped he never got in *People* magazine. He worried it might bring him bad luck.

But Pepper was worrying anyway. He loved Roxanne and he hated bringing her to this horrible place at this horrible time of the morning. A dozen times at the motel they had just come from he had almost told her to call the whole thing off. Let's keep the baby, he had wanted to say. It will work out. Who knows? He might grow up to be President of the United States.

Of course, Roxanne was convinced she was carrying a girl.

Pepper couldn't believe his bad luck. Roxanne was the second girl he had gotten pregnant in the last two months. Betty Sue McCormick had been the first, and boy had that been a mistake. The weird thing about the whole mess was that he hadn't even liked Betty Sue. Yet he had gone out with her a dozen times and had slept with her twice, once before he was involved with Roxanne, and once after. The second time had been the real killer. He had had no intention of even talking to her again. He was no two-timer, never had been. But then she had called and told him to come over, and before he knew it he was on his motorcycle, flying down the streets. She was home alone and wasted no time in taking off her clothes and his. But afterward he got out of there as fast as he could. He went home and showered for half an hour. Just the smell of her on him had made him feel unclean.

She had laughed as he left. She said, "I've got you now."

Then a week later Betty Sue came up to him at school and told him she was carrying his baby and was a few weeks pregnant. She must have conceived the first time they made love. She looked so happy that he was sure she would insist on keeping the child. But then she cackled when he asked her about her plans. "Don't worry about Salt, Pepper," she said. "She's not going to live to a ripe old age."

He hadn't understood that she meant to kill herself along with the fetus. But she committed suicide that very night, and whatever guilt he felt about her death, he felt twice as much relief. Sleeping with her had been like snuggling with a maggot. She was bad news, that Betty Sue. Their child would probably have grown up to be a serial killer.

The tall stern doctor who was performing Roxanne's abortion suddenly appeared in the doorway. "Call Dr. Kline," he ordered the nurse. "Immediately. Tell him it's an emergency. I want him here in five minutes."

Pepper jumped out of his seat. "Is something wrong with Rox?"

The doctor threw him a weary look. "There are complications. Wait here. We'll take care of it."

The strength went out of Pepper's legs and he had to sit down. The *People* magazine fell off his lap and onto the floor. Something else Betty Sue had said to him the last time they had spoken came back to him right then. He didn't know why. Surely it had nothing to do with Roxanne, and her situation. Yet just the memory of it was enough to curl Pepper into a helpless ball of fear.

"Your seed is like a disease inside me," Betty Sue had said. "It's a catching disease. I might cough and give it to someone else. I might do that on purpose. I'm sure whoever catches it next will die."

"Please, God," he whispered. He thought if Roxanne died, he would die with her. She meant that much to him.

He never knew how right he was.

For Roxanne Wells, better known as Rox, the doctor had been gone only a little while. Not the long time she imagined *before*. But what was that before, she asked herself? Suddenly there was something in her mind she couldn't quite put her finger on. A memory that was more than a memory, and somehow less. Something long and complex. How odd that she should forget it altogether, especially when it had just come to her. It was as if she had gone to a movie and then been asked immediately afterward what the movie had been about. And she responded, "I can't remember." Not a single scene. All she would know is that she had seen a show.

It must be the shots they gave me, she thought. I am not losing my mind. It is not the end of the world.

Ah! Something about the end of the world. That's what her strange dream had been about. She remembered then that Leslie, Stan, Helter, and Pepper had been in it. Plus Betty Sue. Poor Betty Sue. She should never have killed herself. What a waste of life, she thought. Life was so precious.

But this time Roxanne did not notice anything peculiar in the fact that she could contemplate the sanctity of life while simultaneously cutting short the life of a fetus. The strange liquid feeling in her guts continued to grow stronger. It wasn't painful, just odd—like her dream of the end of the world. All these things could have been happening to another Roxanne. She was just lying there on her back with her legs up in stirrups—watching colored images on the fluffy white clouds that drifted by. She didn't feel like a direct participant in the drama.

But the drama was just getting started. The doctor returned and he looked worried. He began to work on her again, and when he lifted his hands to collect another surgical instrument she was surprised to see that his plastic gloves were soaked with blood. He swiftly strapped a blood pressure wrap on her arm and pumped it up. His black eyes grew big.

"Roxanne," he said. "How do you feel?"

She yawned. "Dreamy. Am I almost done?"

He reached for a bottle of solution and a fresh needle. "Have you ever had any trouble with excessive bleeding?"

"Like a hemophiliac?"

"No." He stabbed the tiny bottle with the needle and then stuck the needle into the I.V. "You can't be one of those. Hemophilia only affects males." He put a hand to his head. "This has got to have a reason."

"Huh?"

"Just relax."

"All right." She couldn't be bothered talking anyway. She felt too sleepy. A nice nap right now sounded wonderful.

Then she felt a stab of pain deep in her guts. It's suddenness was matched only by its fury. It was as if someone—a witch maybe with long red hair and bony fingers—had taken a knitting needle and poked her right through the belly button. Roxanne felt her heart skip as the pain throbbed from her midsection into her head. She let out a bloodcurdling scream. The doctor jerked upright. The mean nurse came running through the door.

"Where is Dr. Kline?" the doctor snapped.

"He's on his way," the nurse said. "Is she going to be all right?"

"Not if we don't stop this bleeding." The doctor reached for a swab of cotton balls. He picked up a scalpel. "We have to prepare for anesthesia. I'm going to have to open her up."

Open me up, Roxanne thought? That didn't sound good. But at least her pain was receding swiftly, as quickly as it had come. She didn't know if it was because the doctor had pumped more medicine into her I.V. or because whatever it was that was wrong inside had already burst open and the pressure had been relieved. She just hoped the river running from the broken dam was not filled with her blood.

For the first time, she wondered if she was going to die.

And just that thought was enough to crack open the entire world of death. Betty Sue whispered in her ear. You can get up now, Rox. You can walk out into the waiting room and drive back to Salem with your Pepper and pretend that you never tried to murder your baby. But you will find few people there, only those who have displeased me. Those who are already as good as dead. Then you will watch them die, one by one. Until I come to you again in the black night in the form of Queen Beetle, and put my needle in your belly, and make you bleed again, and again, and again. Until you realize that I am a devil so powerful even God leaves me alone to play as I wish.

Roxanne sat up and pulled her legs out of the stirrups. The doctor and nurse did not mind. They continued to work frantically with a reclining bloody mess that seemed to have little to do with her. Roxanne scooted off the table and reached for her clothes. Her green medical gown was filthy with dark stains and she was happy to be rid of it. Once dressed in her own clothes, she felt much better. She stood up and walked out of the room, without even a glance back. But she thought she heard the doctor saying something to the nurse like, "We're losing her." She didn't care. She was remembering what had happened the last time she had changed her mind about having the abortion. Suddenly she remembered the whole story. She had written it all down, after all, and never mind what that bitch Betty Sue thought.

Pepper was sitting huddled over in his chair when she opened the door to the waiting room. He was crying, and at first she thought he was upset about a story he had read in the *People* magazine that was lying at his feet. But then she realized that Pepper never cried. Not unless . . .

It was then she understood that he was crying about her.

Roxanne whirled around and looked down the hall, back the way she had come. Off to her left she could see the doorway that led to the operating table, where she knew the doctor and the nurse continued to work frantically on her. But straight down the hall, near the end, the walls had begun to elongate, stretching the hall into what could have been a pathway into infinity. The way vanished into an awesome blackness. She glanced back and forth, between her weeping boyfriend and the unknown void, and it would have been easy to step into the waiting room and take Pepper's hand and return to Salem. But she knew Salem would not be there, at least not as a city filled with people. If she chose that route, she would once more step back into Betty Sue's wicked reality. Yet there was nothing in the void that drew her. In fact, its sheer awesome-ness frightened her. She wavered at the doorway, uncertain. Something Betty Sue said came back to her right then. Words in Betty Sue's bedroom, at the end of the story.

"That is the difference between you and me. You had only one story to tell. I have millions."

Betty Sue would just torture the five of them all over again, Roxanne thought. The witch would mix up the plot, and the suffering would come at them from different and unexpected directions. It was a hopeless path to go to Pepper, she saw, much as she wanted to. Yet she desperately needed to talk to him, just once more, if only to say goodbye. But she knew she couldn't without great risk. She knew if she so much as stepped into the waiting room, as she had done before, they would both be caught in Betty Sue's web. There was nothing to be done, and it was so terribly sad.

"Goodbye, my love," she whispered to him. She had said too many goodbyes for one day. Her heart heavy, she turned and walked back down the hallway. She scarcely paused as she passed the operating room. The doctor had exhausted all his skills. The nurse was calling out the poor girl's blood pressure readings. The numbers were sinking fast. Blood soaked the floor in dark puddles. The doctor stopped and stepped back from the table as if he were afraid that whatever inexplicable fate had struck his patient would strike him next. He ripped the surgical mask off his face and wiped at the sweat pouring into his eyes. The numbers went flat. The girl's eyes were closed, her face composed.

"She's gone," the doctor said solemnly.

"I am going," Roxanne said. She walked forward, and the first steps were the hardest. She thought of all the things she was leaving behind, and was almost tempted to retreat, to go around the circle one more time with Pepper and her friends, even if it meant unimaginable suffering. But then suddenly, unexpectedly, the darkness softened. As she reached the supposed end of the hall, and passed beyond it, she was encompassed in a wonderful light, where she saw many rich colors and heard many wonderful sounds. Sounds that had nothing to do with the hymn that Betty Sue had sung to catch her unfortunate butterflies. In that moment Roxanne felt as if she had stepped into the center of all things, where the light of the stars shone bright, and the ending of every story was joyful.

Pepper heard Roxanne's scream of pain but remained in his seat, praying feverishly. He did not understand how things could have gone bad so quickly. Everything he read about abortions had said it was a relatively easy procedure. Once more he cursed himself for putting Roxanne through such torment. He swore when he got her out of there he would make it up to her if it took him the rest of his life. He was very serious about her. From the first night they had gone out he had thought she would one day be his wife.

Several minutes crept by. They could have been hours. Then Pepper thought he heard Roxanne's voice. Even more strange, as he glanced up, he thought he saw her standing in the doorway that led back to the operating rooms. But it couldn't have been her because he could see right through her. When he blinked she was gone. Yet the sound of her voice hung softly in the air. So soft that he heard it in his heart and not with his ears. A whisper of love. A whispered goodbye.

"Rox?" he called.

Goodbye my love. Be wary of the witch.

Pepper got up and hurried through the door. He didn't care what the nurse and doctor said. He had to find out what was happening to his girl.

He found out all too soon.

She rested on the operating table, her legs down from the stirrups, her lower body covered with white towels that slowly turned dark red as he looked on. Her face was pale beyond belief and she lay as still as a fallen statue.

"Is she dying?" Pepper cried and stepped into the operating room.

The doctor looked over at the nurse. "What is he doing here?"

"Come on, son," the nurse said, taking him by the arm. "You cannot be in here. The doctor is working."

Pepper shook her off and stepped forward. The doctor wasn't working anymore. He had already given up. He was covering Roxanne's face with a sheet now. Pepper reached out and stopped him. He touched her red hair, the side of her cold face. She lay on her back with her eyes closed. Pepper leaned over and listened at her lips for the faintest sound of breath. But he couldn't even catch a whisper of life.

"Oh, baby," he moaned and put his arms around her, and hugged her, and kissed her. But she didn't stir. "Oh, Rox, what have I done to you?"

The doctor put his hand on Pepper's shoulder. "I'm sorry, son," he said with feeling. "I don't know what happened. She just started bleeding and I couldn't stop it. I've never seen anything like it."

Pepper stood up straight and looked at the man. "She wanted to keep the baby, you know. I talked her out of it."

The doctor nodded. "I understand how that must make you feel, but you couldn't have known this would happen."

Pepper thought of Betty Sue. How she had also died after being with him. An unseen curse was at work here, he thought. It would come for him next. He only prayed it didn't wait long. He deserved to die. He glanced one last time at Roxanne. She had been the best thing that had ever happened to him.

"Yes, I should have known," Pepper said.

Pepper walked out of the operating room and left the clinic. He got in Roxanne's car and drove home. It was early, still pretty dark. He drove fast and didn't see anyone on the highway until sunrise, when he spotted a hitchhiker standing beside the road in the middle of the desert. It was a young woman, with long red hair and a black cape that reached to her feet. He didn't want to stop for her. The loss of Roxanne lay heavy on his heart, like a mountain of frozen lead. But the girl was alone, and he feared she could be in danger once the sun was in the sky and the temperature rose. He pulled the car over to the side of the road. He watched as she collected a black bag at her feet and slowly walked toward him.

"Can I have a ride?" she asked, leaning in the open passenger side window. She was attractive. Her red hair shone like a torch and her green eyes danced as she spoke. It was funny, he thought, she even looked familiar, although he was sure he had never seen her before. He would have remembered someone like her. She smiled a mouth full of white teeth. "Please?"

"Sure." He leaned over and opened the door for her. She climbed in and set her black bag on the car floor between her black boots. "Where are you heading?" he asked.

"Salem," she said.

He put the car in gear and they rolled forward. "That's where I'm from. I can give you a ride there, if you'd like."

"Oh, I'd like that very much."

"How did you happen to be out here in the middle of nowhere? Did your car break down?"

"No." She giggled. "It caught fire. I was barely able to get out alive."

"That's a shame." He fought back a spasm of grief. He was not going to cry in front of a complete stranger. It was going to be hard having company right now. He forced himself to offer his hand, and he had to fight to keep it from shaking. "My name's Pepper."

She squeezed his hand. Her touch was cool and slimy. He assumed she had recently rubbed some kind of lotion on her skin. "I'm Beetle," she said.

He took his hand back quickly. "Is that a first name or last?" Not that he cared.

She grinned. "It's both." She opened her black bag and began to take out an assortment of odds and ends. She lay them on her lap: a cigarette, two bullet shells, an open razor, and a stainless steel fork. Pepper followed her actions out of the corner of his eye. She picked up the fork and played with the metal prongs with the tips of her fingers.

"You know," she said. "I appreciate your giving me this ride. I'd like to make it up to you somehow." She paused and stretched her body into a more upright position. "Could I cook you dinner tonight?"

Pepper shook his head. He knew he wouldn't be eating today, or tomorrow for that matter. He couldn't imagine doing anything for the rest of his life except thinking about Roxanne. What was he going to tell her father?

"I'm sorry," he said. "I'm busy."

She nodded, then smiled, as if he had said yes instead of no. Then she reached over and poked him in the side with her fork. It hurt, and he jerked the wheel and almost sent the car off the road.

"Hey!" he said. "Stop that."

"I'm sorry," she said sincerely. Then she was silent for a moment, before saying, "Are you sure I can't talk you into it?"

He wished he hadn't picked her up. "I am quite sure."

She smiled again, unconcerned. Once more he was struck by how familiar she looked. That brilliant red hair—there was something he was missing here. He was confident in time he would remember where he had seen her before. He watched as she picked up her things and put them back in her black bag.

"And I am quite sure I will change your mind," she said sweetly.

They drove toward Salem.

Look for Christopher Pike's

Chain Letter II: The Ancient Evil

CHRISTOPHER PIKE was born in Brooklyn, New York, but grew up in Los Angeles, where he lives to his day. Prior to becoming a writer, he worked in a factory, painted houses, and programmed computers. His hobbies include astronomy, meditating, running, playing with his nieces and nephews, and making sure his books are prominently displayed in local bookstores. He is the author of *Last Act, Spellbound, Gimme a Kiss, Remember Me, Scavenger Hunt, Final Friends 1, 2,* and *3, Fall into Darkness, See You Later, Witch, Die Softly, Bury Me Deep,* and *Whisper of Death,* all available from Pocket Books. *Slumber Party, Weekend, Chain Letter, The Tachyon Web,* and *Sati*—an adult novel about a very unusual lady—are also by Mr. Pike.